D0046259

NIGHTSHIFT

NIGHTSHIFT

A Novel

Kiare Ladner

MARINER BOOKS

Boston   New York

HarperCollins books may be purchased for educational, business, or sales promotional use. For information, please email the Special Markets Department at SPsales@harpercollins.com.

Originally published in the United Kingdom in 2021 by Picador, an imprint of Pan Macmillan.

FIRST U.S. EDITION

Library of Congress Cataloging-in-Publication Data

Names: Ladner, Kiare, author.
Title: Nightshift : a novel / Kiare Ladner.
Description: First U.S. edition. | New York, NY : Mariner Books, [2021] | Originally published in the United Kingdom in 2021 by Picador, an imprint of Pan Macmillan.
Identifiers: LCCN 2021031408 (print) | LCCN 2021031409 (ebook) | ISBN 9780063138247 (hardcover) | ISBN 9780063138254 (trade paperback) | ISBN 9780063138261 (ebook)
Subjects: LCSH: Female friendship--Fiction. | LCGFT: Novels.
Classification: LCC PR6112.A3335 N54 2021 (print) | LCC PR6112.A3335 (ebook) | DDC 823/.92—dc23
LC record available at https://lccn.loc.gov/2021031408
LC ebook record available at https://lccn.loc.gov/2021031409

ISBN 978-0-06-313824-7

22 23 24 25 26 LSC 10 9 8 7 6 5 4 3 2 1

For Greg

Some are Born to sweet delight,
Some are Born to Endless Night.

WILLIAM BLAKE

PART I

1

At its peak my obsession with her was like a form of self-harm: a private source of pain and comfort.

When I found the ring box in the back of the drawer, I didn't want to open it. Navy and heart-shaped, it has a finely brocaded border and thin silver hook. The lining is pearly satin indented to hold a delicate jewel. A market seller provided it for a sard ring I'd bought, shoving the chunky band determinedly into the slot. I could've saved him the trouble; I'd no need for the box, yet was captivated by its fairy-tale charm. On leaving the stall, I slid the ring onto my finger and smoothed the satin back into a tight clasp.

For almost two decades, I haven't looked at what's inside the box. Simply having it in the room will hopefully pull me through my task. When doubts hover close, I move it about restlessly. I place it behind my computer as if its reliquary power can channel through the screen, or hide it far away on the windowsill by the moldy coffee cups. Getting up from my desk, I pace the room with it in my palm.

Since being unable to sleep, I've passed through a shadow curtain. The present has become dark and stagnant; the past circles vividly around me. Sharp memories cut through chronology's thin skin. In the strange energy of these insomniac nights, I have begun to write as consolation. To make a story that will put an end to reliving flash fragments, to remembering only the most troubling details.

Easily, I slip back to the day I first saw her. I had a job in media monitoring; we provided clients in cars and construction with daily updates of press content. The articles were selected by senior analysts; my work was to write the summaries. Given that copying out the opening paragraphs brought no complaints, I wasn't motivated to do much more.

Excused from staff meetings due to client deadlines, I'd twirl about in my office chair. Shutting my eyes, I'd picture the second floor, open plan and strip-lit. The boards separating cubicles decorated with photographs of loved ones, families, and pets. One neighbor's neat lineup of sharpened pencils, another's orderly stack of camomile and fennel teas. My desk strewn with tire-related articles, my board pinned with ideas for me and Graham, my boyfriend. The drawn conference room blinds meant I didn't need to picture my conventionally dressed colleagues. Who were, in turn, spared the sight of me: a woman in a faded sweater and jeans with a mid-length tangle of orange hair.

No matter how often I played the game, when I looked again my surroundings would be both as I'd visualized them and not. The concrete materiality of the objects was identical but the colors, the quality of light, the atmosphere were subtly different. *See,* I'd tell myself, *you don't know it all. Things change. You can't predict how they'll seem in thirty seconds, never mind till the end of time.*

One August morning with sixteen months to the end of the twentieth century, I was more wrong than usual. When I blinked back into the room, a new person was seated opposite me. She didn't appear to have noticed my twirling around in Megan Groenewald's world—but while I'd have noticed her anywhere, in east London suburbia she was like an exotic zebra fish that had swum off course.

She wore a short, black-and-white, Bridget Riley–type number. Her build was lean, long-limbed, and coltish; her hair was a shallow sea of inky curls. She had fine, straight features and close-set blue eyes so dark as to glint like pitch. I wanted to introduce myself but the cords that looped from her ears to her Walkman put me off.

Since she was typing like a demon on her keyboard, I flamboyantly increased my own speed. When my document contained more errors than words, I glanced at her. She lifted her head; she had a slight squint.

"I'm Meggie," I said.

"I'm Sabine."

"What are you listening to?"

She took her earphones out. Her hands trembled as she passed them over to me; her nails were bitten to such small tabs that her fingers seemed entirely made of skin.

Surprised she didn't mind me sticking her earphones in

my ears, I listened. An expressive male voice sang tenderly to a sweeping accompaniment. Wiping the earphones off with my thumbs before handing them back, I said, "I like it."

"It's 'La Chanson des vieux amants' by Jacques Brel."

"Are you French?"

"Belgian. Jacques Brel is Belgian."

"No," I said. "Are *you* French?"

"Belgian," she said, "but yes."

Then she added, "Also German, Jamaican, Jewish, Egyptian. It's a long story—"

"You don't have to go into it."

"Thank fuck. I hate this question."

"People ask me all the time too."

She frowned. "If you're French?"

"No, where I'm from. When I say, *South Africa*, they say, *Don't you miss the weather?* I wish I could press a button to answer them."

She cocked her head to the side, biting her lip. "You are how old?"

"Twenty-three."

"Me too."

We looked at each other.

"I don't know much about Belgium," I said.

She shrugged. "It's flat. How about South Africa?"

"Parts are flat, parts are mountainous. Growing up there in the eighties . . ." I hesitated; she waited. "I knew things were wrong. I felt it as a child. But I didn't fully understand. Now I do but I'm here."

What was I getting at? Speaking about this could be awkward. The music from the earphones in Sabine's hand had changed to a tune with a strong beat.

"It's complicated," she said.

I nodded. Ten minutes later, an apple jelly bean clipped my shoulder. When I looked up Sabine had popped her earphones back in. Her English was almost perfect; the tone of her voice was mesmeric and low. I sucked the tart sweet slowly.

For the rest of the day, I imagined conversations in which I said the things I wished I had and asked the things I wanted to know.

2

Sabine wasn't a big talker and my fantasies of meaningful conversations stayed no more than that: fantasies. If she'd hinted at intimacy in our first chat, she rebounded from it afterwards. Yet had she distanced herself from me consistently, I'd have lost interest. Instead, right from the start, there was a push and pull between us. We had moments of sudden openness, affinity even, and their promise kept me hooked.

Many of our exchanges centered on food. Every day Sabine brought in a cooked dinner. She put it in the fridge in the morning. At lunch, she heated it in a pot on the hot plate. By the time she ate at her desk, the whole floor smelled of her meal.

One day, the CEO and the HR director came to our office for a meeting with clients. As they left, the CEO wrinkled his nose and looked around. Sniffing suspiciously, he walked down the aisle between the desks.

He stopped when he got to Sabine. "That smells delicious."

"It's *cuisse de canard confite*," said Sabine.

The HR director said hastily to the CEO, "I sent round an email, and we removed the microwave. She must have used the hot plate—"

"Duck leg?" the CEO said.

"Candied," Sabine said. "Would you like to try?"

"Don't mind if I do."

She took a plastic fork from next to her takeaway coffee mug and gave him a taste.

He chewed slowly, swallowed, and nodded approvingly. "Takes me back to a fabulous meal I had at the George Cinq Four Seasons Hotel."

"I know it," said Sabine.

"Are you from Paris?"

"No, but I lived there. I worked near the Four Seasons."

"What work did you do?"

"I was with Crazy Horse. You have heard of them?"

The CEO looked goggle-eyed.

I put "Crazy Horse" into Internet Explorer.

One of the secretaries called the CEO to the phone. "Wonderful to meet you," he said to Sabine. "Next time you're at our Victoria offices, drop in for a chat."

According to the internet, Crazy Horse was an upmarket strip show.

After the CEO and the HR director had left, I said to Sabine, "Wow. You made an impression."

She shrugged and put some more duck leg in her mouth.

I said, "Working at Crazy Horse must have been quite something."

She seemed to be studying me. She took a long, slow sip of water.

Then she said, "I never worked at Crazy Horse."

"You didn't?"

"No," she said. "But now I get to heat my *cuisse*."

Another day, Sabine was late with her meal. When I went into the kitchen, I noticed her shadow on the wall; it was slinky and elongated, like an Aubrey Beardsley sketch. She was wearing a peacock-patterned halterneck dress; all she needed were some feathers in her hair.

While she stirred a rich black ale, onion, and beef stew with a wooden spoon, I asked, "If you weren't at Crazy Horse, where were you before here?"

She stuck a finger in the pot to test it. "Sunset Strip."

Sunset Strip in Soho was known for being a more empowering strip joint. For having women-only nights too. I'd read about it in a London listings magazine. I could easily imagine Sabine there but I said, "You're lying!"

She smiled.

"Seriously, what were you doing?"

"Baking bread."

"You're just saying that."

"Why would I just say that? Baking bread is cool. You work through the night. You play loud music. You take drugs. You go for drinks in the morning—"

"So why did you stop?"

"The head baker was hassling me. It was a small town by the sea, the kind of place where you can't get away from somebody. One morning I left and didn't go back. In London, it's easy to disappear."

"Sure," I said. "But, why media monitoring?"

She lowered the stove's dial. "Why did *you* choose it?"

"I was staying with family friends in Telford. Doing a crap job—"

"Like this, then."

"Crapper. For a company on an industrial estate that bashed out dents in cars. I answered the phones all day. *Dent Mend and Paint Repair 01952 746—*"

"You remember the number?"

"On my deathbed, it'll still be going round my head."

She laughed.

"Telford wasn't for me," I said. "I grew up in a parochial town."

"Meaning?"

"Narrow, insular. Once, they had a beauty contest in a shopping mall. Anyone could go on the platform, enter themselves. The crowd booed or cheered. If they booed, you came down again. The audience was mostly black people but the winner was a ghostly blonde in a settler's dress. And her prize was . . ."

"Yes . . . ?"

"Two cartons of cigarettes!"

"No wonder you're done with towns," Sabine said. "But how did you end up here?"

"The people I was staying with knew someone in media monitoring. They thought it'd be better than temping. How about you?"

She scooped her stew efficiently onto a plate. "The day I saw the ad in the papers, a psychic told me Ilford was in my stars." She licked the spoon, then shrugged. "Who am I to fight destiny?"

Usually I came into the office earlier than Sabine and left before she did. But one afternoon, I hung around. I'd thought of asking her for a drink; if we left together, the conversation might head that way.

As she packed her Tupperware into her lime manga rucksack, I said, "Your food always smells intriguing."

"What do you mean?"

"Smells good. What was it today?"

"Moroccan tagine." She pulled the drawstring closed.

Tossing my small denim handbag over my shoulder, I followed her to the lift. "I'd love to go to Morocco," I said.

"I went with my lover once," she said.

"Lucky you." I wondered if it was a woman or a man.

The lift arrived, empty.

"And lucky him," I tested.

"Lucky *her*," she said, giving me a look as she stepped inside. She pressed the button. "We went to Fez. It is like in the fourteenth century. We stayed in a palace with an old pool."

"I'm jealous."

The lift descended.

"Fez is a sensuous place," she said. "You walk in the medina. You go through the dark alleys. You get lost. Around one corner there are perfumes, these perfumed stones the women rub on themselves. Around another corner, you see a tannery, you smell the piss they soak the skins in. And around another corner, you go through a side door into a marble palace."

I stared at her in wonder.

The lift doors opened.

"I'll send you the recipe for the tagine," she said.

3

If Sabine's talk was elusive, it seemed to me free; if it was fanciful, it fed my image of her as a brave heroine in a dark fairy tale. I was awed by her ability to be herself—unconventional, uninhibited—where I'd never had the courage to do the same.

Negative space is the lifeblood of obsession. In the late

nineties, I felt as if I was mostly negative space. Although I wasn't the daughter my mother wanted, I'd never had the guts to rebel. She said I was like my father: passive, meek, defined more by what I bumped up against than what I chose.

An English lecturer, romantic, and dreamer, my father was killed in a car accident when I was two months old. Before his death, my mother was a professional ballroom dancer. The way she told it, she'd had tremendous potential. But finding herself a widow with *an extremely demanding baby*, she gave it up. Taking out a loan, she opened Renata's Roses & Blooms. She hired a trained florist, Thandi, who did most of the work.

My mother's many unquestioning acolytes regarded her as a sparkling force of nature. She could be charming, creative, and charismatic. But she also had a deep store of anger within her. In public it occasionally darkened her face, though the thunderclouds only broke when she had me to herself. Unfortunately, with it being just the two of us, this happened often, her fury shaking our tin-roof house as loudly as a pelting of hail.

The outbursts would be followed by tearful apologies. Then by platitudes that made no sense. Then by suggestions of renewed intimacy that I had to comply with if I didn't want the anger to return. Huddled under her sunshine quilt, I'd be asked to tell all, in particular about boys. It took many naive confessions before I realized that our intimacy depended on my being the person she wanted me to be, not the person I was.

After I failed the law degree my mother expected to lead to a solid career, or at least a distinguished lawyer husband, I escaped to the UK. As a child, I'd buried myself in books; during the wasted years spent trying to memorize legal cases, I'd had no time to read, but in Telford I began to crave fiction again. I longed to lose myself in other lives, to feel the pulse of other worlds.

Yet the impetus to register for a part-time English literature degree came, unexpectedly, from cocaine. A guy at Dent Mend gave me a tiny "takeaway" to try at home. I made three dots (there wasn't enough for lines) to share with my hosts' sons. We claimed it had no effect but late that night, sleepless and bursting with bravery, I filled in the registration forms.

I'd assumed that my father's genes would breeze me through the course. But to my surprise, studying a subject I thought I'd love didn't come easy. Getting a grip on theoretical arguments was tough. Nonetheless, I persisted in organizing my life around it.

In a leafy south London suburb, I took a room in a house-share that was private, professional, and quiet. Nights I didn't stay over at my boyfriend's, I got up at four A.M. to work. After scraping through Post-colonialism (just), I moved on to Victorian Gothic. But I was a slow reader, a distracted thinker; when I came across lines I liked, I'd mull them over for hours . . .

Despite my approach leading to flights of fancy rather than academic completion, I kept thinking I had to steep myself in the spirit of the books. Buying black taper candles on my lunch break, I bumped into Sabine. I told her of what I was trying to do. Later, she burned me a death metal album by Gorguts called *Obscura*.

"This," she said with authority, "will definitely help."

4

One autumn morning, I sat in the light of my black candles attempting to write an essay on *Dr. Jekyll and Mr. Hyde*. After two hours of getting nowhere with Gorguts in my ears, I decided to go in early to work.

Sabine had been off all week with the flu, and I'd volunteered to write her summaries. "Don't bother telling the client," the manager said. "Just do them as if you were her." I affected her excellent posture as I typed in her passwords (XaviToujours, lemortlemort87) and signed off her emails *Sabine Dubreil*.

Doing the extra work meant staying late, but with it being Friday I fancied leaving on time. The next inbound train would give me the head start I needed. After brushing my teeth and splashing my face, I hauled on a shirt with a cerise bow chosen by my mother. My makeup, usually minimal, could be nil; without Sabine around, nobody would notice me.

On the train, I buried myself in *Exquisite Corpse* by Poppy Z. Brite. Though hardly a course book, I allowed it as a public transport treat. By the next stop I was lost in the cannibal killer's New Orleans. The shadow of someone crossed over me, but only when something tickled my ear did I look up.

A white feather was attached to a white wing, which was attached to a lime manga rucksack, which was attached to Sabine. She was head to toe in radiant white: bellbottoms, platform shoes, and a crop top. She grinned; with glitter on her cheeks, she didn't look ill at all.

"You're early!" she said.

"Going in early to do *your* work," I said.

She pulled a shocked face. "That's terrible."

"I know. You're bad."

"Don't go. You can skip it."

"And do what?"

"Come with me."

"Thought you had flu?"

She waved her hand in the air. "What I've got to do matters more than Thomas Telford and Balfour Beatty."

"Really?" I eyed the wings.

"You have heard of Reclaim the Streets?" she said. "The global anti-capitalists?" I shook my head. "They're anti-cars, anti–big corporations. They protest, but in the way of the future. Less of the hairy shirts, more of a celebration."

I stroked the feathers; they were spikier to the touch than they appeared.

"This week is Toxic Planet by Islington Town Hall. In Africa, they've started GM crops. Farmers get the seeds for free but the plants won't fertilize. So they get stuck in a vicious cycle."

I smiled. "Didn't know you were an activist."

"I'm not."

I raised my eyebrows.

She tossed her head. "I'm not dedicated."

"Skiving off work seems pretty dedicated."

"You should see what the others do," she said. "Me? Sometimes, I do it. Get there before it starts, put out the leaflets, set up the tables—"

"Some of my lecturers at university were activists," I said. "I always hoped I'd have been one too. But by the time I was a student, it was our first free election. Then Mandela became president." I stopped; I wanted to show where my allegiances lay but not sound virtuous.

Sabine was watching me. "You can be an activist today. If that is what you want?"

The train windows became mirrors as we passed through a tunnel.

"I haven't got any wings," I said.

"Never mind," she said. "My friend is bringing body paint. She is a gifted artist. We can make you brilliant silver. Or—green?"

The train drew into Shadwell station.

Sabine touched my arm. "Call in sick. Say you caught the bug from me."

I laughed and got up.

"*À tantôt,*" she called, as I went through the doors.

*

Changing platforms, I could feel the pressure of Sabine's touch. Why was I always such a good girl? It was crazy, going in to do *both* our jobs. *À tantôt* was a Belgian expression for "see you soon." I could turn around, go back, make it true.

On the District Line, I kept thinking: get off, switch platforms. But . . . How could I explain? This foreign activism would be wrong for me—laughable, too easy. I'd be an imposter on its high moral ground. I changed trains and changed again until I got to Ilford.

At work, the offices were empty. I thought back to when I was four, my first day at kindergarten. My mother had instructed me never to go anywhere with strangers. When our teacher said we were going for a walk, I told her I couldn't go. She locked me in the classroom. The scent of pine trees blew in through the high windows. I could still see the disintegrated tissue in my hand as I sat in front of my brown cardboard suitcase waiting for everyone to return.

After starting up my computer, I went to Sabine's side of the desk. I sat in her chair. Her workspace was clear: no pens, no coffee mug, no cutlery. Nothing was pinned to her felt board. She wasn't untidy but there were usually a few CDs or pieces of fruit lying about. For a moment, I wondered if she'd come back. What if next week she called in with another illness and then disappeared, like she did with the bakery job?

Staring at her drawers, I recalled my mother snooping among my things. The drama that had followed. *Don't*, I told myself.

In the top drawer was a bottle of Guerlain Shalimar. I

breathed in the dusky scent of dry roses, vanilla, and some unknown essence. Underneath were a carton of menthol cigarettes, a couple of keys, a tube of hand cream, and a diary we'd been given by Volkswagen. I flipped through the pages. There were lightly penciled names: the post guy, the team manager, a woman in bookkeeping. Sabine gave birthday cards to colleagues; this was evidently how she kept track of the dates.

About to close the drawer, I noticed a brown envelope at the back. Blank, torn open at the top, it contained three blurred Polaroid photographs of a man or a woman, I couldn't discern which. A Sabine-like figure. Sabine, after a holiday, sunburnt berry-brown. Or Sabine in male fancy dress; the jeans seemed to have a masculine cut, the short-sleeved shirt too. Or perhaps this was the lover who'd stayed with Sabine at a palace in Fez. He or she was moving, or the camera was moving, or both. What was captured was no more than the vaguest impression; a viewer could invent almost anything to fill in the rest.

Footsteps sounded in the stairwell. After they moved on, I opened the lower drawer, which was deeper with folders hung across it. I flipped them back and forth; one felt heavier. Behind copies of news clippings was a square box with Alexander McQueen lettering.

It contained a choker with an oval pendant. On the disc crouched a jewel-encrusted scarab with a tiny skull head. I turned it over in my palm. The back was inscribed: *My Sabine*.

I fastened the choker under the cerise bow at my neck.

The scarab had heft where it sat in the hollow of my clavicle. For the rest of the day, I didn't take it off. Again and again, I fingered the engraving.

This was how it felt to wear Alexander McQueen.

I didn't give a fuck what wearing designer jewelry felt like. This was what it felt like to be someone's Sabine.

My Sabine.

5

While my days were spent copying out sentences about tread depth, my boyfriend's were spent organizing courses at a community center. Graham wasn't crazy about his job but had more tolerance for it than I for mine. Often he recounted funny stories about his colleagues and went for after-work drinks. He fitted them in despite (ironically, but successfully) doing a part-time diploma in law.

Although he'd suggested we try studying together, being at his place distracted me. When he wanted to discuss it, I put the discussion off. With his approaching twenty-five, I worried it might lead to the subject of living together. We'd been going out seven months: we liked and were attracted to each other; sex, talk, and intimacy came naturally to us. Obviously, we'd struck it lucky—but the topic stuck like a fish bone in my throat.

If I moved in with Graham, I'd surely never leave him or he me. Which was great, of course it was great. Except, I feared that'd be it. Trapped in a life I hadn't quite intended, I'd never be able to change, to know myself beyond the stencil of my upbringing.

Besides, there were times when a small, unexpressed part of me yearned for another kind of life, to be another person, even. Once, walking home from Telford train station, I passed a pulsing derelict house bathed in ultraviolet light and longed to go inside. Another time, dancing alone in my room to a Lacuna Coil CD I'd bought in imitation of a woman in the queue at Tower Records, I felt as if my fingertips were touching the edge of another world . . .

Yet when I watched classic films with Graham on his worn leather sofa, my perspective wavered. Much as wilder moments attracted me, the pull they exerted passed. In our different ways, what we both wanted was similar. We shared values and interests but also each had our own dreams. What I ought to do was tell him about lives that intrigued me. If I told him of my longings, he'd tell me his in turn.

So late one November afternoon, naked in bed with a bottle of red wine, I told Graham about my colleague, Sabine.

After I'd described how she looked, how she talked, and the places she'd traveled, I said that she'd worked in bread. They'd baked through the night, done drugs, and gone to the pub in the morning. Graham didn't look impressed. I recounted the time with Sabine and the CEO and the *cuisse*. He wasn't impressed by that either. Then I told him she was part of a global anti-capitalist movement. If this impressed him marginally more, it was all the encouragement I needed.

"Sabine's the coolest person I've ever met," I said.

"Ever?"

"Everything about her is strange and beautiful. From her blue-black squinty eyes—"

"She's squint?"

"On her, it looks good."

"Right," said Graham.

He strained his face to aim both eyes at my nose.

I swatted him with a pillow.

"We don't talk much," I said, "but if I catch her with a far-away look, I pelt her with a jelly bean. Same if she catches me. Sweet start to a friendship, huh?"

He raised an eyebrow. "A friendship?"

"I hope it becomes a friendship."

At university I'd slotted into groups I had little in common with. When unable to keep up my cheery image, I'd let connections lapse. In London, I'd hung out with South African acquaintances until they left to teach English in Taiwan. Then I'd piggybacked Graham's social circle. Fearing intrusiveness, with women especially, I ran at the slightest hint of confrontation. In sexual relationships, I felt safer.

Graham tickled his fingers across the freckles on my shoulder. "Meggie . . . ?"

"Normally I make friends with people who befriend me first," I said. "It's time to start choosing."

Graham slipped on top of me. I liked the feeling of his

long lean body pressing into mine. He gave a cheeky smile. "Like you chose me?"

"*You* chose me."

"*You* were checking me out at the pool table. My mates were like, *See that cute gingerhead with the brown, puppy-dog eyes—*"

"Sorry, Mr. Brown-Haired Dude with brown, puppy-dog eyes yourself. You came on to me, remember?" I rolled us over, so that I was on top of him. "*Would you, um, like to go to the cinema or, um, maybe something else, sometime, if you're free?*"

Graham thwacked my bum.

I grabbed the wine from his bedside table; a single drop fell into my mug.

"More in the cupboard," he said.

I flung open his wardrobe door: the neat shelves of folded jeans, ironed T-shirts, pants, socks. "No wine!"

"Kitchen cupboard, Meggie!"

On my way to the kitchen, I stopped off in the bathroom. While I peed I thought: *Sabine would pee with the door ajar.* I wished I'd left the door ajar. Peeing could be sexy. What else would sexy Sabine do? But in the utilitarian ex–council flat kitchen with its linoleum floor, venetian blinds, and Graham's sister's wedding photo on the fridge, I lost her vibe.

Back in the bedroom, filling my mug from a bottle of rum (I hadn't found wine), I tried to explain Sabine again. I described her clothes: a baby-blue shift dress with a sailor collar, a brown-and-yellow circle skirt, black velvet trousers and an oyster-pink jacket. I said how I'd once seen a Vivienne Westwood label sticking out of her shirt. When I asked her about it she'd laughed. She said it was a fake, that all her clothes were. She bought them on Petticoat Lane.

Graham yawned.

"You're bored?" I said.

"We've been on the same subject for hours."

"One last thing, then. She remembers everyone's birthdays but when I asked about hers, it had been the previous day— and nobody'd noticed!"

"Incredible."

"It's in my diary so she'll get something from me next year."

"Very conscientious."

"I'm not trying to be conscientious."

Graham yawned again. "You fancy her."

"What d'you mean?"

"Seriously, Meggie. If I went on about the bloke at work's enviably squinty eyes and how his birthday was in my diary and there was a sweet jelly-bean game going on between us?"

"Women aren't scared of being fascinated by other women."

"Sure." He swirled the rum around in his mug. "I just don't get it, though. What about her is *that* fascinating?"

I sighed. "Haven't I been telling you for hours?"

He rolled his eyes. "Feels like days . . ."

I sipped my rum, moist-eyed and snubbed.

"Hey, come here," he said. I snuggled up against his chest

and he stroked my hair. "Maybe it would make more sense if I met her?"

"Mm. In the meantime, I could cook you her intriguing tagine."

"Can't wait."

"Fine, I won't, then." I curled away.

"Don't be like that." He yanked me back.

"I wouldn't mind getting one of those clay pots to cook it in," I said. "You know the ones that look like a hat?"

It wasn't the first time I'd spoken of a meal I intended to cook. On the food front, I was both a terrible chef and a dreadful procrastinator. The latter quality was more to Graham's advantage than he knew. He said, "I could get you one for Christmas."

"Please! Graham!" I made guttural vomiting noises. "Don't ever get me cooking shit for Christmas!"

"I was joking, Meggie."

"Sorry. It's just, I hate Christmas."

"I know."

I refilled our mugs. "Sabine's going clubbing on Christmas Eve. A warehouse rave at a secret location. You phone a number on the day to find out where it is. I overheard her telling someone else."

Graham took a few contemplative gulps of his rum. Then he put our mugs on the bedside table. As he leaned close, his floppy cowlick fringe brushed my forehead. "Talking of Christmas, I'm not doing anything nearly as exciting as Sabine but . . . I wonder if, um, you maybe, um, fancy coming

8888

8

back to my sister's place in Scotland with me, um, maybe, sometime, if you're free?"

6

If I *had* chosen Graham, I reasoned, then I ought to be able to choose Sabine.

Having turned down her toxic-food protest, I needed to make the next move. Other non-cool people at work befriended her easily. I saw the post guy, who peppered every second sentence with "hey-ho," chatting to her in the kitchen, just her and him there for ages, then her hugging him. Or the placid middle-aged bookkeeping woman who referred to Sabine as her daughter; Sabine didn't mind, they lunched together regularly. One day, she even blew Sabine off. Sloping wearily to our desk, she apologized, saying she'd forgotten a client's meeting.

"No problem," said Sabine—and my moment had come.

"D'you fancy lunch with me?" I asked.

"OK."

"Where were you planning to go?"

"Greggs bakery. Then a walk around the Exchange."

I hated shopping malls. "Great! We can do that."

She laughed. "No, let's go to Valentines Park."

"I've never been—"

"You've worked here how long?"

"I know."

"Valentines is the best thing in Ilford," she said.

Waiting downstairs for Sabine, I put a couple of coins in a call box. I rang Graham at work to tell him about the Valentines walk.

"*Comme c'est romantique!*" he said.

"You go to the park sometimes," I said.

"Don't call to tell you."

"Maybe you should."

"Hn."

"Should I be worried about your secret days?" I said.

"*Very* worried," he said.

"What secret thing are you doing now?"

"Reading *Fairer, Faster, and Firmer: A Modern Approach to Immigration and Asylum.*"

"Are you jealous of me, then?"

"Of your next hour, yes. In general, no."

"If it were in general yes," I said, "I'd take you for supper to make up."

"You could work on it."

"I have to work on it *and* take you out?"

"I'll take you," he said. "Stockpot at seven?"

Stockpot was a place in Soho that served seventies-style comfort food with a handwritten three-course menu that cost the same as one course anywhere else. I knew already what each of us would have. Graham: three-color salad starter, me: avocado vinaigrette; Graham: chicken fiorentina and veg, me: poached salmon and veg; Graham: rice pudding, me: golden syrup sponge with custard.

Usually I liked Stockpot, but as Sabine breezed out of the building with her powder-blue scarf wafting behind her, I wished Graham had suggested somewhere sophisticated and French. In (Belgian) French spirit, I said *"à tantôt,"* blew a kiss down the line, and hung up.

Valentines Park was ten minutes away. Walking there, we listened to Fauré's *Requiem.* It was Sabine's suggestion; she wore one earphone, I the other. I'd not known her to listen to classical music before but she said it was the only thing for Valentines. Perhaps the music was responsible for the serious mood that came over her.

As we strolled through the grounds, past the ponds and canals, the green and coppering shrubberies, she told me that a poor family called Valentine had lived in a cottage here. Then the estate was bought by *quelqu'un* in 1696 after her husband, the Archbishop of Canterbury, died. The mansion was built for her. In the eighteenth century, another *quelqu'un* gave the grounds their features, and thirty years later, Charles Raymond—

"A nice name, no?" she said.

"Nice when you say it." I pursed my lips for my best French impression.

28

"Charles Ray*mond*," she said, mocking my imitation, "bought the estate and made it more Georgian style. He planted the Black Hamburg vine. It was destroyed but a cutting lives on at Hampton Court. They gave it the name Hampton Court vine."

"Original," I said.

"In the nineteenth century, a Roman stone coffin was found here. Then, the council opened it as a park. It has been public for almost a hundred years. In the First World War, Belgian refugees stayed in the mansion. After the war, it was a convalescent hospital so that's why there are ghosts."

"Ghosts?"

"Yes, you believe in ghosts?"

"Not sure," I said. "My mother who is alive haunts me more than my dead father."

She took my hand. "When did your father die?"

"Before I can remember. I was a baby," I said.

She kissed my hand and let it go.

"How about you?" I said. "D'you believe in ghosts?"

"Of course. I come here to be near the ones who died."

"In the hospital?"

"No, my own ghosts. From my own life."

"Who are they?"

She acted as if she hadn't heard; I was sure that she had losses greater than mine, of people she'd known and loved.

"Why were there Belgian refugees?" I asked, since she seemed more comfortable with her potted history lesson.

"When Germany invaded, they had to flee. A quarter of

a million came here. Agatha Christie met one and invented Poirot." She turned to me. "If you write a book, I can be your Belgian."

"I'm not going to write a book."

"But you love to read?"

"That's different."

"I love to read too," she said.

"What do you love to read?"

"Thomas Mann, Goethe, Shakespeare, and Proust."

"OK," I said. "Maybe you will write a book then?"

She laughed.

After nothing more was forthcoming, I asked, "What happened to the refugees?"

"At the end of the war, Britain sent them back. The government gave free one-way tickets. Their story was forgotten. An old priest told me."

"A priest?"

"He comes here a lot. He tells me things, then forgets, then tells me again." She shrugged. "I feel sad for old men on their own."

"Not old women?"

"No," she said.

She took out a joint. I knew what she meant: it was easier to feel sad for people who weren't like you. She lit the joint, had a toke, and passed it to me. I had a toke too.

As a layer peeled off the day, I noticed the trees differently. How magnificent they were, how old and dignified. While their leaves chattered high above us, I felt as if I'd slipped into an English storybook from my childhood. I put the flat of my hand on the knobbled bark of what Sabine said was a hornbeam; I ran my palm along it.

Sabine put her hand on the bark too, and then on top of mine.

"Come," she said. "We need to go back. But first, the wishing well."

The wishing well wasn't what I expected. It was a squat dome-shaped concrete structure embedded with flints and quartz. Sabine said fifty years ago children would scratch a wish on a leaf and throw it in. She sat scribbling on her leaf; I tried to see what she was getting down but it was indecipherable. I simply wished for us to be friends.

I thought my wish would come true. But in the days following our walk Sabine was increasingly aloof. She didn't take her earphones out when we talked and responded to my questions with the briefest of answers. When she caught me looking at her, she looked away. I raked through the day at Valentines, trying to work out what I'd done. Finding nothing, I became sure that she saw how hungry I was to know her, to know about her, to be close.

In the local library one rainy lunch break, I came across a leaflet on the park. It contained all the information Sabine had told me. But libraries were often the haunts of old men. The priest had probably come here and read it; he'd passed the information on to Sabine who'd passed it to me. The other possibility was that there was no old priest. But there was no reason for me to choose that explanation.

In early December, I found a book still in its bag on my desk: *The Healing Energies of Trees* by Patrice Bouchardon. When I asked Sabine about it, she said she'd liked it and thought I would too. I wasn't sure what the gift meant. Was it my turn to make another move? Or was it the closing seal on our friendship? Ending relationships, I'd always paid for the last meal, or parted ways after I'd given a gift rather than vice versa. I didn't want any chance that the other person could feel used.

Although this was a friendship, I imagined Sabine was doing similarly. Her gift was about saying no nicely. Hurt, I left the book at the back of my work drawer. Reining in my glances, I tried to look forward to the Christmas holidays in Scotland.

7

The day before Graham and I left for his sister's place in Inverness was the day of the Christmas do. Ordinarily I avoided work drinks, but since the Christmas ones started during office hours, they were pretty much obligatory. I found myself hemmed in at a trestle table with colleagues I hardly knew. Wondering how long I'd have to stay, I heard, "And Sabine's off to do nightshifts at London Bridge."

"Sabine *Dubreil*?" I asked.

"Yes," said the matronly woman to my right.

"She's only been here four months!"

"I know, it's a shame," said the woman.

"Got to move on for the CV," said the ex-army head of finance.

"How will nightshifts be good for her CV?"

The hot guy from IT shrugged. "Different job, innit?"

While he doled out generous refills of Sauvignon from the bottles on the table, I scanned the pub crowd. Sabine's lime rucksack was easy to spot; she was the only woman in a group of men by the bar. After draining my glass, I excused myself.

She was mid-conversation with the best-looking director, the one who with a lot of imagination could look a little like Richard Gere. I tapped her shoulder. The pub was loud. I yelled in her face, "You're changing to nights?"

"Yes," she yelled back.

"Why?"

"I'm not a day person."

I nodded; I could smell her perfume, her smoke and mint breath.

"Are you a day person, Meggie?"

"No," I said. "Not at all."

"So you must do nights, too."

The director tapped his shiny brogues. He put his pint down heavily; the froth spilled. *I was wrong about* The Healing Energies of Trees. *I interpreted her gift wrongly.*

I considered asking the director for a transfer then and

33

there, but it didn't seem like quite the right moment. When he started talking as if I was a midge he wanted to bat away, I mouthed *"à tantôt"* to Sabine and left.

Until I heard of Sabine's move, working nights hadn't occurred to me. But over a Christmas break more toddler-centered than I'd anticipated, the idea took hold. On Graham's sister's computer I checked the schedule. Fourteen nights on, followed by fourteen nights and days off. Parents changed their body clocks for the sake of their sprogs. Surely, I said to Graham, I could do it for the sake of my studies?

If the rationale sounded disingenuous, Graham wouldn't question it; he thought my academic efforts were linked to my late father's career. The misconception wasn't my fault, though nor was it easy to correct. I'd told him I didn't miss what I hadn't known. But over the years I'd noticed that people who came from ordinary, stable families didn't believe me.

Usually I was careful not to take advantage but in this case the truth was complex. It wasn't just about working with Sabine; it was about doing what she had done. Inverting the notion of living by day seemed subversive. She'd slipped stream, and invited me to do the same. If I turned it down would I ever get the chance again?

The first weeks of January were grayer, rainier, and more drab than usual. The essay I'd been trying to write was stuck.

I hadn't heard about my application for nights. And Graham was pissed off that I wanted to do them so much.

"What about us?" he said. "Shift work's shit for relationships."

"Shit work's shit for relationships too," I said, crabbily.

And shit work it was, shittier than ever. Without Sabine around, my tolerance for the job was shot. My whole life seemed to be a cycle as tedious as my summaries of tire news.

One morning while my colleagues were in a meeting, I stared despondently at the staff photo board. We'd been asked to bring in pictures of ourselves as children and Sabine's was still there. Above her name tag was a child of eight or nine. She was onstage, dressed in a midriff top, hot pants, and boots. Her mouth was stained bright red as if she'd been eating raspberry sherbet. She was the naughty little girl I'd always wanted to know. The girl I'd been discouraged from inviting home. *A sexualized child*; I could hear the words in my mother's disapproving tone.

I looked at the photograph above my own name: my dorky orange pigtails, my pinafore dress, my shiny brown buckle shoes. Then I took the thumbtacks out and, not caring that it didn't make sense, I swapped the photos around.

Of course, it was only after I completely gave up on hearing about nights that a letter came through the internal post. I can't recall where the interview was held. It may have been the Victorian warehouse near London Bridge where the nightshifters worked; by day it would've seemed a different place entirely. All I remember clearly was being sure that I had botched it—but I was wrong. Either that or there weren't as many people clamoring to invert their body clocks as I'd imagined.

By the time I got home, there was already a message on my phone: I was to be at the London Bridge warehouse at ten P.M. the following Monday to start the job.

PART II

8

As instructed, I entered the warehouse building through the cracked glass door. Going up two dirty flights of stairs, I came into a vast workspace with a concrete floor, exposed brick walls, industrial-size bins, and glue-stained desks. On some of them were bulky out-of-date computers; on all were stacks of white paper, newspapers, glue sticks, and scissors.

I scanned the room for Sabine but there were no familiar faces; the unfamiliar ones looked sallow and waxy in the fluorescent light. I was told to trail someone called Earl, a mini Muscle Mary with breath like a firelighter. His hair was in twists dyed gold and he had one gold-capped tooth. He explained that my job would involve reading the papers to find and summarize articles to do with crime. I'd send them out to government clients by six o'clock each morning. He'd show me the ropes but I'd have to figure out the specifics myself.

"Unfortunately, your predecessor's not available," he said.

"OK," I said.

"He topped himself," Earl said.

"God."

"I know. The shift leader still feels bad."

"The shift leader?"

Earl put a finger to his lips. "He was *always* calling in sick. One day, she made a voodoo doll from screwed-up newspaper and stuck pins in it. She did it as a joke but then . . ."

He raised his eyebrows.

"I'll be careful about calling in sick," I said.

"No, you'll be all right," said Earl. Then he added, "So long as you don't take the piss."

We were by the sink, making coffees. Looking for a sponge to wipe the grubby mugs, I saw maggots at the drain. Earl called over the shift leader. She wore her fine black hair in plaited buns that she shook hopelessly. "I keep telling the management."

Earl filled a quarter of his coffee mug from a clear bottle with a Cyrillic label. "Vodka. Want some?"

"Vodka and coffee?" I said.

"You don't have to have the coffee," he said, smiling.

"Maybe later," I said.

"Won't be a later," he said.

After I'd stirred the coffees, Earl introduced me to Lizard, a guy in a leather jacket worn scaly at the seams, and then to Coño, the nightshift dog. Lizard told me Coño was actually Earl's.

"Nice name," I said, patting her. "I haven't heard it before."

Earl and Lizard doubled up laughing. "You've not been to Spain?"

"Not yet," I said.

They cracked up again.

"It's 'cunt' in Spanish," said Lizard.

"Hey, hey," said Earl. "It's not the same thing, it's the language of love."

"Thought that was Italian," I said, and they stared at me like I was a square peg.

A woman with breath to rival Earl's put her arm across my shoulders. Her hair was bottle mahogany-red with a short pull of gray at the roots. It gave off an oily scent overlaid by a cloyingly sweet perfume. Her green eyes were clumpily mascaraed and shattered by red veins.

"Ignore them, babes," she said. "I'm Sherry. Let's hand out the coffees."

I don't remember much else from the night other than an overall impression that I'd gone too far, I'd made a mistake. I'd traipsed after Sabine as if she were the Pied Piper. And where was she now? As for me, I seemed to be alone in a land of losers, wasters, and misfits.

9

Night after night there was no Sabine.

At the end of another day's struggle to sleep, I'd set off from my houseshare in the dark. Slamming the front door shut, I'd sense my cohabitants' collective flinch. Disregarding it, I'd head down lonely streets past glowing windows. At the station I'd cross over to the empty inbound platform. I'd get a train that was harshly lit, though scarcely a quarter full.

Disembarking at London Bridge, I'd continue against the flow. Each day had a particular feel to it. Sunday was low with the weight of the week ahead. Monday was simply dogged. Tuesday, a smidgen lighter. By Wednesday, the spirit began to change. Thursday sparkled with the weekend's approach. Friday was carefree, careless, positively ebullient. Saturday sat deep-seatedly in the comfy fat of the weekend. Even being out of sync, the cycle was affecting, reinforced by its effect on my colleagues' moods too; getting buffeted by the day world was unavoidable for any of us.

Leaving the station concourse, I'd pass a taxi rank, then turn off the main drag. The darkness seemed denser here than where I lived. The streetlamps were often broken, the neighboring buildings abandoned or shut until usual working hours resumed. Except for the one with the cracked glass door.

I'd go in. And up.

Up two flights of stairs to a static buzz and brazen lighting. To grubs and broken chairs and filthy keyboards. A constant supply of farts emitted by who knows who, a blocked-nose-worth of paper dust. Drinking mud-thick coffee to stay awake, I'd scan the newspapers for *murder, accident, assault, crime, prisons, arson, harm, rape, death, die, died.* I'd snip, glue, and type. Photocopying summary packs, I'd count the mechanical flashes of light. I did it automatically with my fingers, only keeping track of every tenth flash that passed.

Between tens, I'd think of nothing. My sleep-deprived mind would blank; I'd stand.

Around two A.M., I'd eat Pot Noodles at my desk like everyone else. Bombay Bad Boy. Beef and Tomato. Hot 'n' Spicy. Pot Mash. Pot Curry. Chow Mein. If there was a delay due to a late paper, or a problem in the print room, I'd sneak out to the petrol station kiosk. With crisps or a strawberry milkshake or an energy drink for a final boost, I'd go down to the river's edge. Leaning over the cold, concrete barrier, I'd relish the stolen moment off.

Back at the warehouse, the night would burn on. When it finally thinned, I'd feel the end's approach viscerally. Like a sportsperson trained to play to the exact length of a game, I squeezed out the last of my efforts. I emailed my summaries to clients and deposited my press packs in the courier's boxes: HOME OFFICE, PRISONS, CPS, POLICE.

Slinging my denim handbag over my shoulder, I called, "See you later" to the emptying room.

Whoever was left echoed "See you later" back.

10

"Still here," Lizard noted when I'd passed the mid-shift mark.

"One of us, now," said Earl.

"Les Misérables," said Lizard.

"Nah," said Earl, "Les Stuck."

I hoped they were wrong. And also hoped soon to hear a

more authentic French accent. Earlier through the stairwell window, I'd seen a woman in a brown raincoat emerging from a yellow convertible. Though her face was obscured by a patterned brown umbrella, I was *sure* it was Sabine.

When by Pot Noodle time she hadn't materialized, I finally approached the shift leader. She shook her plaited buns: she'd never heard of anyone by that name. I checked with Lizard, who said he hadn't either. Earl said she might be a newbie on the opposite team, the ones who did the work during our fortnights off. Maybe I was wrong then, maybe I hadn't seen her. "Maybe she's *my* opposite?" I said.

"Yours is a twenty-stone bloke," said Lizard.

"Who's been doing the job for as many years," added Earl.

I wondered out loud why Mr. Twenty-Twenty hadn't shown me the ropes.

"He's in Bangkok," said Earl.

I gathered then that with this job when you were off, you were off—and I couldn't wait.

Working nights made me feel unexpectedly constrained. You never got to say, "See you tomorrow"; it was always, "See you later." You never got the blank slate of a fresh, new day. My press packs were shoddy; my clients continually complained. The shift leader said not to worry, that I'd improve with experience. But, since my body was incapable of sleep by day, I hardly intended to give experience a chance.

Instead, I promised myself to look for other work once the fortnight was up. I promised the same to Graham, whom I'd not seen since starting because it was all I could do to get by.

With my autopilot gone AWOL, I expended my energy on instructions to put food in my mouth, smear soap over my body, stand under the shower until it washed off, and then lie pointlessly in bed.

One night, I leaned back against a concrete pillar in the toilets. Doing something I've never managed before or since, standing dead upright I fell asleep.

Sherry shook me awake. "Babes, are you all right?"

"I'm fine," I said, embarrassed to be caught off guard.

"You're sure?"

"Just tired."

"Come to the pub after work."

"I don't fancy drinking in the morning."

"Sorts out the sleep problem," she said. "Mother's milk."

At the basin, I ran the cold tap full volume over my wrists. A teacher at school had said this would cool your blood supply. Perhaps cooler blood would make me more alert.

Instead a bump against my hips jolted me. Winking at my reflection in the mirror, Sherry said, "We could be sisters! You and I!"

Sherry was the off-grid version of the day-job woman who'd called Sabine her daughter. Had Sherry called me her daughter, it might have been OK. But, sister?

I kept the water running hard while she tra-la-la-ed down the corridor.

11

The last day of shift, I managed a miraculous four and a half hours' sleep. Emerging from survival mode, I blow-dried curls into my hair, depilated the rest of my body, and generally spruced up. My plan was to head to Graham's for some A.M. intimacy after work. But around midnight, in the corridor by the photocopying room, someone grabbed my arm.

"You've changed to nights too?" Sabine's cheeks were flushed.

"Yes!" I said.

We stared at each other.

"I guess we're on different teams," I said.

She nodded. "I'm at Energy downstairs."

"I didn't know there was a downstairs."

She slanted her eyes at me.

I said, "I mean, I didn't know anyone was there."

"You never go to the pub?"

"Not so far. Maybe today."

"No," she said. "Today is . . . on the roof."

"The roof?" I said.

"A celebration," she said. "Exclusive."

"I forgot, I can't today," I said.

"It is your last shift?"

"Yes."

"You have to come, then." She smiled.

I slowly smiled back. "OK, I'll come."

She made a zipping sign across her mouth.

Turning to hide my grin, I rushed off to finish my work.

Most of the team had left by the time I was done. A few had asked if I was going for drinks and Earl had replied, "She never does." It'd be a surprise for them to see me on the roof—if they'd been invited, that was.

The staircase ended at the sixth floor, which seemed deserted. After going through several double doors I wondered if I'd be able to get back. Ready to retrace my steps, I noticed a shaft of dusty light. A short flight of stairs led to a door jammed open with a brick.

The roof was a flat expanse of black tar. The dawn sky blazed red through oyster frills of gray cloud. Older lower buildings were still in the dark while higher glassier ones flashed beams of sunlight. The railway track was one kind of break in the city's density, the broad shimmering curve of the Thames another.

Sabine was at the far end, smoking a cigarette.

I went over to her. "Was the celebration called off?"

She inhaled deeply, cheeks hollow.

"I guess obviously it was," I said.

I put my hands in my bomber jacket pockets.

Sabine was shivering in black leggings, black boots, a black sweater.

"Sorry I'm so late. I'm just unbelievably bad at—"

"Shhhhh." She put a finger on my lips.

For a moment, I was confused.

Then she leaned in and kissed me.

Her mouth was a toasty combination of toothpaste and cigarettes. I could smell the scent at her neck. I was responding to her almost before I realized. The feel of her kissing, her tongue and mine, was softer than any I'd ever experienced.

But then I pulled away. "I can't—" I shook my head. "You know I've got a boyfriend."

"So?"

"I'm not a lesbian."

"Me neither."

I frowned.

She said, "I like both." She stepped back. "You don't like both too?"

"No," I said. "I'm sorry, if I . . ."

She flicked her cigarette dismissively. It had burned to the filter. She put it out in a paint tin filled with butts. "Like the view?"

"Yes. Do you?"

"It makes me feel, how can I say?"

"Alive?"

"Destructible," she said.

"Destructible?"

"We're so small, Meggie. Just small animals who stay in small buildings, do small jobs, go home on small trains. We fuck, eat, sleep—"

"Can't wait to do more of that," I said.

"Sleep?"

"Yes."

She laughed. "Thought you'd say fuck."

"That too," I said, awkwardly. "Speaking of which, I'd better go. I promised to get to Graham's before he left for work." I hesitated; I didn't want to seem weird about the kiss. "Maybe we can swap numbers?"

"I'll give you mine. You give me a missed call."

After keying her mobile number into my new Nokia, I pressed dial. Her rucksack was just a few yards away but I didn't hear ringing.

"You know the way out?" she asked.

"No," I said. "Could you show me?"

"No. But you go down, and right, and left, and left again, and you come to the stairs. Easy-peasy."

Easy-peasy, sure. I was lost in the building for three quarters of an hour. By which time it was too late to catch Graham before work anyway.

12

As the reality of having a fortnight off took hold, my perspective on finding another job changed. Of course nights were hard, but hard for a reason. I was turning my life around.

For the first time ever I enjoyed telling people what I did. *On shift I immerse myself in crime. We read the broadsheets and the tabloids too. Murder, rape, abuse, anything to do with prisoners. You see how the same story is told in different papers . . .*

"Isn't it depressing?" asked Graham's cousin over dinner.

"We-ell," I said, "the previous guy on the job topped himself."

She gasped. "You're happy with your lovely girlfriend doing this, Gray?"

Lovely, friendly, and *natural* were descriptors I wanted to leave behind. Giving the cousin a glinting smile like Sabine's, I moved the conversation swiftly on.

Back at Graham's flat that cold February night, we fought.

"What's with the drunken bravado?" he said.

"You've been drinking too," I said.

"You drink *every* night now."

"Can't sleep. I need it."

"You don't."

"Mother's milk."

He slammed an armful of law books down on the kitchen counter. "Where's this going to end, Meggie?"

Still warmed by the dinner's wine, I went over to him. I hitched up my new stripy skirt. His breathing deepened; it turned me on when he was aroused despite himself. He traced a blue zigzag from my mid-thigh upwards. Just before my knickers, he stopped. "Is Sabine doing nights too?"

I nodded.

He fingered the stretchy material. "So *that's* what this is about."

"She's not on my shift, Graham. I've seen her once."

"But the job was her suggestion?"

"Yes."

He took his hands from my body.

"What?" I said.

"If she says jump, you'll say how high? If she says run, you'll say how far? If she says dive, you'll say how deep?"

I went to the fridge. Graham sounded drunker than I'd realized.

I remembered my mother's accusing me of a sex life before I had one. Holding a bottle of beer, I turned back to him. "If she says, *kiss me* . . . ?"

He shrugged resignedly as if the answer were obvious.

I had the urge to hurl the bottle across the room. Very occasionally, I got these violent impulses. I'd read an article that suggested distracting yourself with a strong physical sensation. Touch a kettle, hold ice, drink water quickly.

I drank the beer quickly, so quickly I felt sick.

We stormed off to bed furious with each other. But my body clock was junked and the powers of mother's milk were limited. In the early hours, I woke up and went down on him. Then he woke up too. In the half-light we were at it like prisoners just released. When he fell asleep again, I lay there and thought: *Yup, I guess it's men for me.*

Yet the conclusion was oddly tinged with regret. And so, because I couldn't sleep, I began to play with myself. As I fiddled, my imagination roamed its usual territory of strong, swarthy guys. But the moment before I came, I overlaid their images with Sabine.

Her heart-shaped face, that smile of hers.

13

My last weekend off, I told Graham I'd cook for him. After printing out Sabine's recipe for Traditional French Moroccan Tagine, I spent the day hunting down the ingredients. These included three I'd never had: goat meat, harissa paste, and argan oil. Argan oil proved the hardest to source. Eventually I found a bottle in the beauty section of a local health food store. The packaging said, "For hair, skin, nails, lips" but the shop assistant said, "Argan oil's argan oil," and I went with her view on it.

The recipe was supposed to take three hours and forty minutes. Since I sawed and hacked rather than sliced and chopped, it took me closer to six. At almost ten P.M., done with timing the meal, I laid the table with my phone by the place mat. Then we sat down to eat.

"This is—interesting," Graham said, his Adam's apple rising and falling.

"Interesting?" I said.

He took another forkful. "What d'you think of it?"

I chewed thoughtfully, imagining a riad courtyard, blue-and-white tiles, little birds flying overhead. "It's exotic."

"Yes," he said. "Pretty rich."

It was exceptionally rich. He selected a few more forkfuls, without the meat. I made myself select forkfuls with meat only. Unexpectedly, my phone lit up. An envelope with SABINE appeared on the screen.

"What is it?" he said.

"Nothing," I said. But, buoyed by the coincidence of the text, I added, "D'you want to know the tagine's ingredients?"

"Go on."

I listed the vegetables first, then the harissa paste.

"Harissa!" he said, as if he'd bumped into an old friend. "Didn't realize there was harissa in it. Harissa's fragrant and delicate."

My phone's screen had gone dark. "Maybe it's drowned out by the goat."

"Goat?"

"You eat meat."

"Sure, but—"

"It really irritates me," I said, "when people think to eat a cow is fine but to eat a goat isn't."

"Does that mean I have to eat every animal on earth?"

"Yes. Or else become a vegetarian."

"Maybe I will. I've been thinking about it."

"Oh, and my meal has turned you?" I picked up my phone.

"It really irritates me," he said, "when people can't stop fidgeting with their mobiles."

"You just wish you had one too."

"Getting one next week for work."

"Oh." I slipped the phone into my pocket. "D'you want to know the last secret ingredient?"

"Definitely."

"Argan oil."

"I've not heard of that."

"It's got to do with goats too."

He looked decidedly sick. "Goat oil? Goat gland oil?"

"No," I said. "It comes from argan nuts."

"Phew."

"Their shells are hard to crack. But in Morocco, goats climb the argan trees and eat the argan nuts. People fish them out of their poo, which has made them softer. They mash them up. And it goes from there."

He stared at me, then started laughing. "You sure know how to sell an *exotic* stew to a meat and two veg kinda guy."

"You need to broaden out." I stuffed more goat in my mouth. Then I put my knife and fork together. "Just nipping to the loo."

"Your broadening out getting to your guts?" he called after me.

"You're gross," I called back. "I need to pee!"

In the bathroom, I opened Sabine's text. It was blank. I closed and opened it again. Same result. I flushed the toilet. If the message was a mistake, I could still send a reply. I turned on the hot tap, then typed: *Looking fwd to seeing you on Mon.* Before I could change my mind, I clicked send.

The mirror above the basin steamed up. I willed my phone

to flash with a return text. But it didn't. Reluctantly, I put it in my pocket and turned the hot tap off.

Graham had cleared the tagine from the living room. In the center of the table was a pack of deflated-looking éclairs. "Got dessert."

"Thanks, Gray."

"I can bring the goat back if you're not finished?"

"I'm done," I said. "It wasn't that great."

"Wait," he said, going through to the kitchen.

"I don't want any more goat!"

But he returned with a bottle of cava. "Not champagne. Though it's good stuff." He poured it out into the two long-stemmed glasses he called the *poshies*, then raised a toast. "To meals together."

As we sipped the fizz, I said, "I've got a plan. D'you want to hear?"

"Plan for what, Meggie?"

"Managing nights."

"I've been giving it some thought myself."

My phone gave a tremor at my hip. "Hang on."

I went to Graham's bedroom. But it had only been a phantom vibration. I buried the phone in my denim bag and applied some lip gloss.

He smiled when I came back. "Glamorized."

"Glamorized," I said.

"So what's the plan then?" he said.

"To live by night only."

His face fell. "You're doing that already."

I shook my head. "From now on, I'm going to be nocturnal in my time off too."

"Ri-ight . . ." He tapped his glass.

"Switching's the problem, Gray. My body clock's screwed. I can't get into a routine. And like you said, I'm drinking—not too much, I enjoy drinking too much, but—too often."

I gave him a moment to say something smug.

When he didn't, I added, "I want to give this job, my studies, everything a chance. This is the only realistic way to do it."

"Realistic, huh?" he said.

Then, without a single *um* or *uh* or hesitation of any playful kind, he said, "The only realistic way to give *us* a chance is if we live together."

I'd thought I was prepared for Graham's suggestion. But with my mind in a panic, I blurted out that I needed time. I wanted to say yes, I told him, but with such a big decision it seemed disrespectful not to take a bit of time.

"How much time?" he asked, in the tone of someone more annoyed than respected.

I promised to let him know by the end of the fortnight. To be at his flat by seven A.M. on the morning I was done.

14

Back on shift, I managed somehow to almost forget about the issue of living together. Whenever my bone-tired mind skirted it, daydreams of dykey inclinations took over. Lying in bed at midday, listless, awake, I'd imagine saying to Sabine, *Maybe I was too hasty, maybe I made a mistake, maybe we could try again?*

Meanwhile, my coworkers were doing their best to help with my insomnia. Sherry brought in thick blackout cloth for my bedroom window. Earl gave me industrial earplugs to mute my housemates. Nothing helped: my eyes burned dryly, my lips cracked, my skin was as sensitive as if I'd been everted. After I heard the tulips at the station whispering, Earl told Lizard, who provided a blister pack of prescription sleeping pills.

The relief at being able to switch off was immense, though the pills had two disconcerting side effects. One was that I still felt foggy when awake: I forgot half my keywords and made careless mistakes. The other was that in the window between taking the pills and falling asleep, I felt hornier than ever.

As the shift progressed, I used this time to experiment with bringing Sabine from the edge of my fantasies to their center. Mostly my impulses slipped into their much-worn tracks. But on the last day of shift, Sabine and I were lying naked together in a warm, muddy rock pool from the beginning of my arousal to its end.

Until then, I'd been no closer to finding an answer for Graham. But in the post-orgasm bath of blissful well-being, I came up with an idea. If anyone asked me to go for drinks in the pub, I'd say yes. And if Sabine came too, I'd play the decision, my sexuality—stuff it, the rest of my life—by ear from there.

The White Hart had green speckled carpet tiles, a wall-mounted TV, a jukebox, and an imitation antique clock with hands stuck on a quarter to nine. It was a traditional pub in every sense, except for its dawn opening and a plastic pink stag's head festooned with fairy lights above the bar.

"What're you drinking?" said Earl.

"I'll get it," I said.

"Wine?" he said. "White?"

"Earl, don't—"

"White wine," he said to the barman. "Large."

"Baby One More Time" by Britney Spears came on the jukebox. Behind me, someone put their hands over my eyes.

"Same for SJ," Earl said.

I wrestled with strong, cold fingers. "*SJ?*"

"You two know each other?" said Earl.

"Of course," said Sabine.

Earl paid up.

Sabine gave a boozy half-smile; I grinned back.

"Oi, lovebirds," said Earl. "Give us a hand."

We took the drinks to the table. As we pulled up extra

stools, I made sure to slip in beside Sabine. Everyone clinked glasses.

"*Salud!*" said Lizard.

Sherry caught my eye. "He's off to Mexico again."

"*Salud,*" I said.

Prawn, a spotty white-blond teenager from the print room, yelled, "*Na zdrowie!*"

"Poland," Sherry said for my benefit.

"Where're you off to, Sherry?" I asked.

"Spain," said Sherry. "Bor-ing."

"Spain's cool," said Earl.

"Yeah, it's cool. He's coming too," said Sherry.

"Which part of Spain?" I said.

"Fuck knows," said Earl. "Wherever."

"We take our vans," said Prawn.

Did everyone here have a van? I wanted to ask Sabine if she had a van. And why she'd called herself SJ. I knew so little about her. But the others seemed to think we were close, and I liked them thinking that.

"What're you up to the next weeks?" Earl asked me.

I didn't want to say, *Sleep, see my boyfriend*—

Sabine stepped in. "We've got plans."

"Plans, eh?" said Earl.

I glanced at his G-Shock watch. My plans to be at Graham's by seven A.M. were fast messing up. I needed to text him but I'd dumped my bag with my phone on the far windowsill.

Prawn took a crumpled fax from his pocket. "Seen this?" He flattened it out. DRUGS WILL NO LONGER BE TOLERATED ON SHIFT.

THE MANAGEMENT. With his pale stubby finger, Prawn under-lined NO LONGER.

Everybody laughed.

"Bloody management," said Lizard.

"That fucker who only did one shift sent forty copies of our bet on the Queen Mother's deathday to Inland Revenue," said Earl. "The managers had no choice."

"Don't worry about it, Prawn," said Sherry.

"Yeah, like I am!"

Earl turned to me. "Want to have a guess at her death date? Costs a pound."

"Sure." It was an excuse to fetch my bag.

"Do it next shift rather," said Sherry. "I haven't got the list."

"What if she pegs it before then?" said Earl.

"Is your date before then?" said Sherry.

"Mine's Wednesday," said Sabine. "If I win, I'll share."

I thought, *I should still get my phone.*

But Sabine pulled me down, her lips at my ear. "I looked forward to seeing you this shift too."

I could smell the wine on her breath. "What?"

She wouldn't repeat her belated response to my goat meal text, but I knew what I'd heard. Just like when a phrase I'd read absorbed me to the extent I forgot everything else, so all thoughts of texting Graham flew out of the pub's diamond-gridded windows. Out into the everyday world where men and women were striding purposefully to work. Their dark suits, their shiny shoes, their strained faces, their neat hair . . .

Inside, I looked at Sabine in her schoolgirl lace-ups,

checkered shorts, and velvet blazer. Lizard, an old-time rocker in his skinny jeans and leather jacket. Earl, with his sharp rave style and Coño sleeping peacefully at his feet. Prawn, moonfaced but energetically punky. Even Sherry, with her ill-conceived glamour, seemed childishly endearing, like a messy three-year-old.

I'd found the tribe I wanted to join.

We were totally, utterly free.

At almost eleven A.M., the pub was about to shut. It would reopen at five P.M. to mirror its trading hours for dayshifters.

Dayshifters.

Thinking back to the game I used to play with eyes closed in my office chair, I went over to the jukebox. Flipping through the carousel of songs, I found Cyndi Lauper's "True Colors." It cost a quid for three tunes. I bought a pack of menthol lights at the bar to get change, then pressed the Lauper button three times. Leaving the song to repeat, I went outside.

The streets around the station had quieted. The morning was wintery though bright. After two weeks in the dark, every color seemed intense. Pink graffiti on the rusty railway bridge. Black branches flecked with lime buds. Overhead, the wide blue expanse of the sky.

Leaning against a bollard, I lit up. I wasn't a real smoker but, inhaling, I rode the head rush.

I didn't notice Sabine until she jostled alongside me.

Stretching out her boyish legs, she helped herself to a cigarette from my pack. I offered to light it for her. The wind blew a few stray curls across her face. She had freckles around her nose that I hadn't noticed before. When the cigarette wouldn't catch, I cupped my hand.

She leaned in; I lifted my head.

Her mouth twitched, showed a dimple. A dare.

I took her unlit cigarette out. Then I kissed her.

Her mouth was soft, her lips the undersides of petals. Though her tongue was strong, our tongues were strong. They moved easily together until hers pulled back, darting, teasing. She tickle-kissed my neck. I tasted her dusky perfume and pressed into her. We grabbed at each other; then stopped, lost in the warm darkness of our mouths.

When the pub door swung open, she began to grind against me. As the team came out, I could feel their eyes on us. The guys watching; the way they were watching. I tugged at Sabine's sleeve. But she drew me closer and kissed more showily.

"Can we talk?" I whispered.

She didn't answer.

With my hands on her upper arms, I moved her gently back; we broke apart.

Our colleagues pretended they hadn't been gawking. They scattered, crossed the road, went to queue at a cashpoint.

I took her hand. It was cold like when she'd put it over my eyes. "Let's go someplace we can be alone," I said.

"What do you mean?"

"D'you live on your own?"

She tilted her head, warily.

"Maybe we could go back to yours," I said.

She opened her mouth, then closed it.

Her eyes became hard glints.

"It's just a kiss, Meggie."

"I know."

"A kiss doesn't mean . . ."

"I know," I said.

My cheeks were hot, my eyes were hot. Whenever I wanted to cry I distracted myself by spelling words backwards. I looked towards the alley. I spelled *snib*. I spelled *ytpme setarc*. I felt her smooth a strand of hair back from my forehead.

In a softer voice, she said, "You don't usually kiss your girl friends?"

"Not usually."

"You're cute. My cute friend who I kiss."

I nodded and swallowed. "I don't know what nights is doing to me."

"Come, now. Everything's fine," she said. "Let's go find the others."

15

Sabine and the rest went on to another pub or a park or someone's flat, but I went home. Later I sent Graham a text. When he didn't reply, I called, I apologized. He asked sarcastically if I'd got lost in the building again. Not this time, I said. There was a long silence. Then I asked if I could come round that evening. I said I'd come early, cook a meal. No, he said firmly. We'll skip cooking, get takeaways.

Guilty, grateful, and off-kilter, I blew a shitload of cash on a bottle of Pol Roger Cuvée Sir Winston Churchill that came in a special wooden box. To accompany the fancy champagne, I'd *have* to give him good news.

I put the fizz confidently in his fridge when I arrived. But instead of drinking it, we launched straight into unexpectedly affectionate sex.

Afterwards we chatted casually, then ate a greedy number of dishes from Jay's Vindaloo. Towards the end of the meal, the bulb in the table lamp blew. When Graham flicked on the main light, the room seemed smaller.

"So, Meggie," he asked. "What's happening?"

I bit at my lip. "Haven't been able to decide."

"I thought as much."

"I'm sorry." Was not moving in with him true to myself, or was it just selfish?

He studied his empty plate. I put my hand on his. He patted it, then drummed the table. "Can't do what you can't do."

Were we breaking up? This easily? This undramatically?

I scraped the bottom of the sag paneer with my fork. A strand of spinach hooked in the prongs. Then I heard myself say, "Graham, I think I might be a lesbian."

"It's Sabine, isn't it?"

"No."

"C'mon," he said. "Crazy-Horse Sabine? Jelly-bean Sabine?"

I shook my head. "She's just a cute friend."

"She sounded more than *cute* when you went on about her clothes and squinty eyes and candied duck and—"

"Things change."

"Who're you into now, then?"

"Nobody."

"Who're you involved with?"

"No one."

He eyed me skeptically.

"You," I said. "That's all."

We were quiet.

Then he shifted in his chair. "Have you ever had sex with a woman?"

I frowned. "That's private."

"But have you?"

"No."

He looked amused. "Really?"

I felt my cheeks redden. "I think about it, sometimes."

"Well, then, Megan Groenewald"—he leaned over to plant a kiss on my forehead—"it's time to do it, huh?"

He started to clear up the empty containers from the meal, putting them back into the takeaway bags.

I thought, *That's it. Over. The end.*

I was tired; the day had been too much. A pathetic snort escaped with a sob.

"Meggie." Graham came over to my side of the table. He scooped his arms looped with curry bags around my waist. I hugged him tightly back. "It doesn't have to be *the end*."

"It doesn't?" I said.

"No." He let me go, then took the bags to the kitchen.

I stood at the door.

Emptying the bins, he said, "You just need to try it."

"And, if I try it? That'll be fine by you?"

"I think so."

"Will you do stuff of your own too?"

"Maybe," he said. "We'll see."

I helped him clear the rest of the plates. I was impressed by his generosity, though even more by his assuredness, his sense of self-worth.

While Graham did the washing-up, I got the videotape ready in the player. The film he'd rented was *The Truman Show*. At the start, the viewer is told that audiences are tired of seeing actors portray artificial emotions. After rewinding and fast-forwarding, I got the tape to pause at the first frame.

Coming into the room, Graham held up a tub with two spoons.

"You got dessert!" I said.

"Always do."

We snuggled on the sofa, eating creamy rice kheer, and I told myself: *So. Bloody. Lucky.*

To Graham, I said, "You know you're sweeter than I deserve?"

16

The following day, Graham left for work experience at a prestigious chambers in Wales. Not having him around made it easier to stick to my intentions. To move away from the everyday, away from the day. To let go of what I knew and push off into the night. Yet pushing off into the night turned out to be harder than I'd thought.

I set a rigid nocturnal schedule with times to get up, run, eat, and sleep. But off shift as on, some internal stubbornness resisted. Without sleeping pills, I lay in bed exhausted but mostly awake. Every few days, I'd pass out heavily, though the short, thick slumbers made me feel drugged: more tired, not less.

When I wasn't maintaining functional necessities, I sat at my desk. As deadlines loomed, my calculations for how quickly I needed to read the course books became increasingly desperate. If I could get through x number of pages in y hours then I'd have z hours for the essay. Night after night, z shrank while I stared into the light of my black candles.

The exploration of my lesbian side didn't fare much better. I went to a bisexual women's meeting in a church hall but the atmosphere was earnest, formal, and conservative. I felt as uncomfortable as at my all-girls school, as much of an oddity as I'd felt then.

It was hardly a fair way to test my sexuality. London had plenty of gay, lesbian, and mixed clubs, pubs, and bars. I'd even seen an advert in a listings magazine for a lesbian sauna. Or I could drop in at the First Out café by Center Point for a baked potato. I liked baked potatoes; I gave myself a date—the date slipped by.

I'd long assumed I did relationships better than friendships. With the few lovers I'd had, I hadn't feared boundaries being crossed. A TV psychologist suggested that for people with authoritarian parents, the bedroom could be where they felt most liberated to rescript their lives. What he'd said stuck; I took for granted that the closeness I'd found with boyfriends could theoretically translate into closeness with girlfriends too.

Yet now I wondered if there was more to my ease with men than I'd realized. When I was with a man, I felt as if I could hide behind my form. The differences between us alone were attractive to him. Whereas in close quarters with a woman, I'd be exposed. If she saw in me what I saw, how could it possibly work? Was it transgression more than lesbianism that I was after?

Whatever I called it, with Sabine its current surged; with Graham, it flatlined. *Cute friend* status meant I had to find new ways to hack the circuit. Living nocturnally was not enough, nor was endless contemplation.

What I needed was to push against myself.

17

Southwark was in darkness. With a power cut to London's central areas, our papers were late; our work was stalled. A note on the warehouse door gave instructions to meet on the roof. I followed the emergency lighting up the stairs. The thump of industrial metal guided me to our crew.

They were sitting around candles in a circle. Sabine patted the space next to her but I sat by Earl and Coño instead. Rammstein's "Du Hast" was playing on the print guys' ghetto blaster. A few people had coffee cups, doubtless half full of spirits, but with it being our first Monday back, the atmosphere was glum.

Sabine wore a blonde faux fur hat and a white appliqué coat decorated with fairy-tale images. Since her hair was hidden, it could have been platinum. The change of frame around her face made her lips seem fuller, her eyes larger.

When "Du Hast" began to warp, the shift leader put it off. The gunpowder night was quiet. Last time I'd been up here, I'd felt surrounded by the city; this time, we could have been floating in space.

"Anyone done anything interesting the last two weeks?" asked the shift leader.

When her hair wasn't in plaited buns, it was loosely crinkled. Her body was angular, broad-shouldered: a swimmer's build. I looked at her wide eyes, her high cheekbones. She had an appealing androgyny. If my fascination with Sabine was about looks, or even nonconformism, the shift leader made for a good rival. Why wasn't I fascinated by her?

"I went to the Noche de Brujas in Mexico," she offered when no one replied.

"Night of the Witches?" said Sabine.

The shift leader smiled; Sabine smiled back.

Fascination was chemical, I thought. But was it my chemicals blending with Sabine's or did she attract everyone as much?

"What d'you get up to?" Earl asked Lizard. "Wittgenstein, Linear B . . . ?"

"Time before last, he shut himself away to read up on the Serbian-Kosovan crisis," said Sherry.

"She's a doll," said Lizard. "Brought me meals—"

"Oh go on, you couldn't call them meals."

"The lasagne, the chili?"

"The Findus Crispy Pancakes?"

A helicopter flew noisily overhead.

"Learn anything that wasn't depressing?" asked a guy from Sabine's Energy team.

"Albania's taking in Kosovan refugees," said Lizard.

"We are too, aren't we?" said the shift leader.

"If you apply for asylum here," said Earl, "it takes nine years to get citizenship."

"Things are improving, though," said Sherry. "Now that Blair's got in—"

"He reminds me of a school prefect," I said.

"Were you a school prefect?" said the shift leader.

"No!" I said. "Were you?"

"Dropped out at fifteen," she said.

"I was expelled," said Sabine. "Twice."

"What for?" I asked, before I could remember to be cool.

"First time, a sex thing. Wasn't my fault but I took the rap. Second time for being a gang leader."

"Don Sabine!" said Prawn.

"I've never led anything but I was a goth," said Sherry.

"Me too," said Lizard.

"I was the darkest goth in town," said Earl.

Everyone laughed. I wished I'd been a gang leader or a goth. But how would my mother have coped? She got angry if I didn't laugh at the right moments in her anecdotes about the florist shop's regular customers.

The Energy guy turned back to Lizard. "If Kosovo was the time before last, what did you research this time?"

Lizard screwed up his face. "Hypnosis."

"That's—different?"

"When I was a kid, my uncle was into it," said Earl. "He'd hypnotize himself, then get me to stick a pin in his hand. Sometimes he stuck one in me too."

"Did you want him to?" asked the shift leader.

"Not really."

"Isn't that, like, abusive?"

"It was the pin, not the penis," said Sabine.

The helicopter flew close again; a candle guttered.

"Can you try the pin thing on me?" said Prawn.

"I've only been doing it two weeks," said Lizard. "And I don't have a pin."

Sherry took a needle from a sewing kit in her bulky handbag. "Ta-da!"

Lizard instructed Prawn to raise his hand. Speaking slowly in a monotonous voice, he counted down from ten to one as Prawn's hand dropped. Lizard picked it up, then pressed the needle into his palm.

Prawn screamed. Staring at the bead of blood on his skin, he went whiter than usual.

"Lie down, Prawny," said Sherry.

Sabine put her hand over her mouth; a hiccup of laughter escaped.

"One of you try it then!" Prawn shouted from where he lay.

The shift leader drew a resolute breath.

Quickly, I said, "I will."

Sabine turned to me; they all turned to me.

"You sure?" said Lizard. "I mean, I don't think I've quite got this."

"You concentrate on the trance," Sabine said to Lizard. "I'll apply the pin."

In fairness to Prawn, Lizard went to more trouble with me. While I lay there with my eyes closed, he told me to imagine an old weather-beaten staircase leading from a cliff to an empty beach. He described descending it, a single stair at a time. Counting the steps down from twenty, he instructed me to relax more completely. *You feel calm, you feel peaceful. You let go. Surrender.*

Sabine held my hand on her thigh. My heart slowed, my breathing slowed, I began to slip away . . .

Then the needle went in.

It felt like I was being branded by a white-hot torch. Scared I would scream a thousand times louder than Prawn, I imagined myself being welded to Sabine.

At last, Lizard started the talk to bring me back. I heard a train; the world felt noisier. When I opened my eyes, the power cut was over. The buildings around us were lit up. Everyone was congratulating Lizard—but Sabine wasn't there. Clenching my sore hand, I felt cheated.

"Back to work," said the shift leader.

As the others stampeded to the stairs, Lizard said, "You'll sleep well tomorrow, Meggie. You went deep."

"How can you tell?"

He gave a conspiratorial wink.

Alone on the roof, I examined my palm; a bit bloody but I'd live. I distracted myself by naming the sights: Borough Market, Southwark Cathedral, the Thames, London Bridge—

"Meggie, we need to fix you up."

Sabine stood in the doorway holding a little green first aid box.

From it she took a Band-Aid, cotton ball, and Mercurochrome. Swabbing my skin, she gave a low chuckle. "Lizard's got a way to go with his hypnosis skills, eh?"

"What d'you mean?"

She stuck the Band-Aid on my palm.

Then she looked me in the eye. "You felt every fucking millimeter of that needle going in."

18

Bolstered by bravery, on my next Saturday night off I caught the train to Charing Cross. Making my way through Covent Garden, I imagined my younger self with me. The thrill she'd have got from being out in London, unaccountable and free. But as I reached the streets near Soho Square, I left her behind. She was too much of her world to understand where I was headed next. Still less, to share my tentative sense of anticipation.

When I found the place, I stood looking at it. I was myself, then I was not myself. Shivering in the early spring cold, I crossed the road to the fat yellow bubble letters above the blacked-out facade. HONEY BAR.

The women on the door wore biker leathers, had spiky hair, and were heavily pierced. As they pointed to an open guest book on a table in the foyer, I realized I needed to write my name. I hesitated.

"Name, name," one of them repeated, speaking loudly the way people do to foreigners.

I wrote *SJ*, then scribbled indecipherably in the box for signature. Parting a midnight-blue curtain, she let me in.

I appeared to be the only woman on her own. The others,

mostly younger than me, were in groups or at least pairs. Taking a seat at the bar, I ordered a Sol. It was what I'd been drinking the night I met Graham. I thought of him playing pool with his mates, the teasing banter between them. Of his lanky body, his soft brown eyes. He was back from Wales tonight; his train would have just come in. What was I doing here?

With my second beer half drunk, I made myself approach a nearby table of girls. One of them, plump with beaded braids, shoved the others along so I could fit in beside her. She asked if I was alone. I said yes. Was it my first time at Honey Bar? Yes. She gave me a warm hug, then asked my name. I said SJ, and introductions followed all round.

As they chatted, I was impressed by how at ease the group was with their sexuality. The girl next to me had come out to her best friend when she was nine. At nine I'd known the word *lesbian* only as a fearful aberration from a story of my mother's about a friend who'd been *turned* by a mannish German bassoon player. I told them my mother's story; they laughed. Afterwards the conversation flowed easily, though much of it was buffered in old friends' banter. It was a relief when they suggested that we go downstairs and dance.

We'd been on the dance floor for only a few songs when a new girl joined us. I didn't hear her name properly. Something like Bitte or Britte or Beata. She'd just come back from a year's volunteering in Malawi. She was tall and Swedish and her skin was very tanned. Her eyes were clear, cornflower-blue. Her body was strong; her features were strong. Her hair was peroxided, freshly cut, schoolboy cut, short back and sides. The kind of cut that begs fingers to run up against the grain.

Shyly, I worked my way next to her. Her style was cool and minimal. I reined in my shoulder grooving, my floppy hands. Getting another beer, I got her one too. We shouted back and forth about Malawi. The lake so big you couldn't see the other side, the awesome fish, the hospital where she'd worked. I'd taken a friend to that hospital, I said. I left out that it was because he got alcohol poisoning. She bought the next beers, and we gave up trying to talk. When a slow song came on, we shifted minimally together. I ran my fingers up the back of her hair. And then we were snogging, beer tongues, beer breath. It was different from snogging Sabine; these were straightforward, lustful, warrior-like kisses.

Several beers past midnight, I found myself stepping across the riverbank onto a narrowboat. After unlocking a door at the helm, the Swedish girl lit a gas lamp and let me in.

"My sister's boat," she said. "She's away for the summer."

The interior was lined in wood; it was simple, everything a bit worn, uncluttered but cozily messy. There were a couple of wicker boxes and some wicker drawers. An elephant-print cloth hung like a curtain to demarcate the living from the sleeping area. To one side was a pine trunk with cushions; to the other, a tatty armchair covered in a brown crocheted blanket. Shivering, I wrapped the blanket around me while she set about lighting the stove. It didn't feel so much like being on a boat as in a forest cabin.

Once the fire was burning, she poured some of her sister's bourbon into mugs. The logs smelled amazing. She said they were applewood. We started kissing again and I felt at ease, content. As I dropped the blanket, she removed my sweater and cami all in one. I took off her T-shirt and bra; beneath them her breasts were luxuriously large. I caressed them, I sucked on the nipples. I yanked my own bra off, grateful then for the chill that made my nipples stand erect. We stroked and kissed and pinched and grappled. Though we didn't speak, my internal monologue wouldn't stop. I kept telling myself she was exactly my type. Hot. Bold. Stunning. But, for all that I tried to talk myself into it, I couldn't seem to get turned on.

Then an idea came to me as clearly as if it were in lights: *Be Sabine.* I changed my posture to Sabine's. I pressed the Swedish girl back against the side of the boat as I imagined Sabine would. Bit and nibbled and teased like Sabine. I enjoyed it; this was fun. But despite losing myself in the performance, I didn't feel the genuine level of arousal needed. When the Swedish girl steered me towards the elephant curtain with the single bed beyond it, I excused myself to go to the loo.

In the tiny bathroom, I fell back on fantasies that usually took me from nought to sixty in two seconds. But they didn't work. I had a pee, flushed, and was about to give up when

I saw the dispenser of liquid cucumber melon hand soap. I pumped some out and smeared it around my crotch.

I don't know what I was thinking because as soon as our jeans were off, we went down on each other. Deliberately, I went down on her first. I enjoyed playing with her; I got caught up in what I was doing, but in a voyeuristic, curious way rather than an aroused one. I took my time, was happy to take all the time in the world. But abruptly she swung herself around and it was my turn.

Breathing heavily, I made noises of appreciation. I tried not to think of what cucumber melon liquid soap tasted like or if it made bubbles, if it lathered and bubbled up. The best, I reckoned, would be for me to fake come before she'd licked all the soap off. I did my Lamborghini quickie impression, making gasps louder than I ever normally would.

Fake panting in the fake aftermath, I pulled her head up to mine. The cucumber melon smelled strongly then; I could taste it as she kissed me, surprisingly tenderly. I felt that I had to acknowledge the soap but didn't know how. She spared me by saying, "You're funny. I like you. But you didn't have to wash down there beforehand."

"I was sweaty," I said.

She said, "I like sweat."

With more gratitude than she could have guessed, I went down on her again.

She was slower now to rise to where she'd been before. As my fingers began to tire, my jaw to get a little stiff, the situation felt familiar. Not as a sexual experience but as something else. I kept trying to place the familiarity. And then it came to me: it reminded me of exercise. Not of running but of how I used to feel when I went to the gym. Repeating the same maneuver, over and over. Getting a bit of an ache but knowing I'd be glad for it afterwards.

When she came, I kept watching her face. Her glowing cheeks, her fringe damp with sweat, her lips just parted. But even at this, her most magnificent moment, even as I was grateful for the privilege to stare and stare, I didn't feel turned on like when I watched a man. Watching a man brought me close to coming myself—again even, if I already had.

Later, I lay cramped up against the side of the boat while she lightly snored. The alarm clock next to the bed ticked. I counted the ticks, wishing I was at Graham's flat where, if I couldn't sleep, I could at least move around. Then I began to wish I was in bed with Graham. The more I thought about it, the more I wanted it; I craved it, restlessly, impatiently.

When the first strain of dawn pressed against the porthole, I snuck out. Closing the door of the boat quietly, I climbed onto the land. I started to walk down the towpath, then accelerated into a run. By the lock I heard someone calling in the distance, "*SJ, SJ.*" I kept going, sprinting up from the canal onto the city's deserted streets. I didn't hesitate or pause or slow down. Only when I reached the station did I realize.

She'd been calling after me.

19

Noisily, I let myself into Graham's flat. The blinds were drawn; the boiler made its reassuring hum. A faint cardboard and pepperoni pizza smell lingered in the air. I put the shower on so the water could heat up.

In Graham's room, I climbed onto his bed. Discarding my clothes, I kissed his stubbly jaw and nuzzled the prickles of his neck. Then I dragged him into the bathroom, under the spray. Kneeling in front of him, I ran my hands up his thighs, following where my fingers had gone with lips, mouth, and tongue.

Afterwards, under the warm, steamy rain, I told him, "I'm not a lesbian after all."

"You tried?"

"I tried."

"How many times?"

"I've only had a few weeks!"

"So?" He kissed the freckles on my back.

"Once," I said, grudgingly. "But it couldn't have had a better chance."

"How so?"

"She was totally my type."

"Your type, huh?"

"My wannabe type," I corrected.

"And what's your wannabe type?"

I slid my hand onto his crotch. "You wanna know?"

I gave him a girl-on-girl story for his fantasies but not the one that had been true. I could still hear the call of *SJ* in my ears. To have given him the truth would have betrayed the Swedish girl too far.

While we stood wrapped in towels beneath the blow heater, I asked, "Is it too early for that Churchill champagne?"

"Meggie," he said, "I've got to get back to Cardiff."

"We'll celebrate another time, then."

"Thought we just did."

I circled his nipple with my finger.

"Ye-es?" he said.

"Let's live together, Gray."

His cheeks were red; I could feel mine were too but we didn't move from the heater's blast.

Then he said, "Got you a little something in Wales."

After rummaging in his toilet bag, he gave me a yellow drawstring pouch. Inside was a circular pendant etched with a squiggly little sheep.

"That's cute!" I regretted the *c* word the moment it came out.

"You like it?" he said. "There were others, more serious, with Celtic symbols and so on."

I ran my thumb over the side of the disc that didn't have the sheep. "You could always get it engraved."

"With what?"

"*My Meggie.*"

Thinking I was making a joke, he burst out laughing. I pretended it was a joke too.

When the hilarity died down, I said, "*My Meggie* sounds stupid."

"That's not what I meant—"

"It's got no gravitas." It didn't compare to *My Sabine*.

"Megan's a beautiful name," he said seriously. "Looked it up when I met you. It comes from Margaret, which means 'pearl.'" I thought of how a pearl forms due to a foreign particle in an oyster. "Pearls have a natural, gentle beauty," he added.

I tugged the cord to switch the heater off. "When shall I give notice on my room?"

"Why not move in when I get back?"

"In two weeks' time?"

We stared at each other, hair half dry, eyes wide.

"If I leave now, I'll catch my landlady before she goes to Ireland," I said.

He pulled me to him; I smoothed his fringe.

"Much as I hate you to go, Mum . . ."

I wriggled away. "Don't ever, ever call me that, Graham!"

He pecked my forehead. "You're so easy to wind up."

PART III

20

Often I am kept awake by guilt. Yet when I truly go back into the past my perspective shifts. As I write the story down, I can see that when I tried to do what I thought I should, my attempts were doomed. How do you treat others decently when you want to become someone else? How do you live well when you yearn to burn with all your spirit in moments of wildness or freedom or excess?

By the April day set for moving in with Graham, I'd been fully nocturnal for almost three months. I'd assumed it would come to feel natural. Instead, the idea of going home to sleep after my last shift began to seem unbearable. Pouring a nip of mezcal by the photocopier machine, Earl asked if I wanted a line of coke.

I thought back to the excitement of the dot I'd tried in Telford. Then I thought of Graham coming round that evening, of the cardboard boxes waiting to be packed.

"Meggie? Yes, no?"

The mezcal burned like a fuse down my throat. "Yes, please."

The dust in the warehouse gave me a blocked nose. While

Earl chopped up the coke with a razor blade, I took a squirt of my decongestant. He made two perfectly even lines. Like in the movies, I gave him a fiver. Not like in the movies, he asked for a squirt of decongestant too.

Together we filled our clear nasal cavities with the numbing white dust. I recognized the bitter taste, the widening sense of possibility. Snorting the last traces back, I said, "I don't come to the pub more often because I'm trying to . . ." *Write an essay on problems of representation.* "Write."

"You're a writer."

"Maybe, one day."

"If you write, you're a writer," Earl said.

"I'm not writing," I said, reining in my lie. "Just trying."

"I mix music. The others do stuff too. Sherry designs jewelry—"

"Hang on—you're a DJ?"

"A trier, as you'd put it," he said. "We're all triers here."

The first line of coke was like taking baby steps in high platform boots. The second made me feel as if I could strut my stuff into the daylight. The third, combined with backing out of the building's shadow into the morning sun, gave a hit of euphoria that not even being a *cute friend* in supermarket sneakers could dim. On the contrary, when I saw Sabine it seemed crazy that I'd been hurt by . . . what? I'd rejected her, then she'd rejected me. Neither of us wanted a proper relationship. Why not embrace the kissy friendship? Why not have some fun!

Sabine checked my needle-punctured palm, then kissed it, though kissy kissing wasn't in the cards. When she leaned in at the pub door it was only to ask, "Can I get some of what you've had?"

"Coming up!"

Sourcing the dealer's number from Earl, I placed an order that made my overdraft bulge. But when, forty-five minutes later, my delivery arrived like a pizza from a guy on a bike, I felt cool, I felt rich, I felt generous: I felt free.

After our crew left the pub, we went to what might have been a common or a heath. A breezy between-seasons place with tufty grass and a marbled sky. While we sat around drinking spirits from polystyrene cups, Sherry said, "I hear you're a writer."

"Nooo." I scowled at Earl.

"Nooo?" said Earl.

"What're you writing?" Sherry asked.

"If I say, I'll spoil it."

"You have to keep it in?"

"Yeah." I took a hefty gulp from my cup.

"Like the multi-orgasmic man," said Sabine.

"Exactly," I said, though I didn't know what she was talking about.

"You mean, tantric stuff, SJ?" said Sherry.

"From the Taoists," said Sabine.

"Taoists," said Sherry. "Oh."

"If a man keeps his ejaculation in when he comes, he can come many times."

"He comes without cum?" said Prawn.

"It's in his imagination," said Sabine.

"Who wants to come in his imagination?" said Prawn.

"He has an orgasm for, maybe, ten minutes—"

"But in his imagination!" said Prawn.

"You take the piss," said Sabine. "But it's *beautiful.*"

"*Beautiful* for the woman too," I said, speaking from my imagination.

I borrowed Earl's blade to cut some wonky lines that he refined. We all snorted them back.

Prawn made a bright moue in his pale, spotty face. "How d'you do it, then?"

"Not easy," said Sabine. "You need to learn the technique. I bought a book in Berlin."

"There's a city I'd go back to in a heartbeat," said Lizard.

Then Sherry said, "Meggie, you've got a boyfriend, right?"

I nodded.

"And he does this ten-minute-orgasm stuff?"

"Not this boyfriend."

"This boyfriend? You have another?"

"No."

"Only Gra-ham," said Sabine mockingly.

"There've been others," I said.

"She likes more than one!" said Prawn.

"What's Graham like, then?" said Sherry.

Everyone was watching me.

"He's sweet," I said.

Prawn said, "If a girl ever says Prawn's sweet—"

"No danger there," said Lizard.

Earl pulled a face. "Sweet, Meggie?"

"I don't know. He's not right for me." I needed to stop. "Things just sort of happened." *STOP, Meggie.* "And then, they kept happening. And, you know when you're in a relationship that keeps going because you don't get round to ending it?"

I sat there shocked. But wasn't I saying the truth?

"I was married to a guy twelve years for that reason," said Sherry. "Lost more than a decade of my life to riding the wrong pony."

"He wasn't sweet, Sher," said Earl.

"He was at first." The cloying scent of Sherry's hair was strong as she leaned close. "Before the jealousy, and the, you know, abuse."

"That's hardly Meggie's situation," said Earl.

"God, no," I said.

Prawn topped up our cups.

"Graham's a good man," I said, hoping to compensate for my disloyalty. "We're not right for each other but there's nothing *wrong* either. He's generous. And mature. And he gives me freedom—"

"An open relationship?" asked Sherry.

I shrugged. "Sometimes I go with girls."

Sabine looked up.

"By 'go with,' d'you mean fuck?" said Prawn.

"Yeah," I said, "fuck." This was true too, wasn't it?

"I'll be generous and mature, any day!" said Prawn. "From now on, I'm only going to be generous and mature."

"Shut up, Prawn," said Lizard.

"Why me?"

"You're giving me an earache, that's why. Your voice is a fucking earworm."

"'S true," said Earl, chortling. "Before I fall asleep, all I hear is Prawn's voice."

"Cunts." Prawn stormed off into the trees to take a leak.

The crew was silent.

Then Earl said, "Sounds like Graham's not enough for you, Meggie."

I could feel Sabine's eyes like a hot beam on my cheeks. "You're right," I said, "he's not. The relationship's not. I ought to break up with him. I'm definitely going to—"

"Used to say it all the time," said Sherry. "*Mañana, mañana, mañana.*"

I shook my head. "Mark my words: I'm going to do it today."

Sabine's dimple was flickering. "Mark my words?"

Then she leaned in and kissed me.

21

Waking up in Graham's bed suggested I hadn't broken up with him. I felt sick in every way: puke-sick, guilt-sick, gut-scared-hungover-sick. The white blinds were pulled down to keep out the light. But the sun wasn't even trying to get in; it was already overhead. My phone was on the pillow beside me. 11:07. Tuesday. Twelve missed calls from Graham (yesterday). I tried to curl into a ball but the skin at my knee pulled; a red-black graze glared.

I recalled the nauseating odor of a plastic apple hanging in a taxi, then getting out, falling onto gravel.

At the bedside table was a glass of water on a coaster. A box of acetaminophen was balanced on top of it so insects couldn't fall in. If Graham dumped me this was how it would be: kind, considerate, and neat.

Had he dumped me?

Unable to find my clothes, I took a faded green T-shirt from his drawer. The scent of his fabric softener stirred me uncomfortably. Usually when he went out he left a note. There was nothing in his bedroom. I went into the study, the front room, and then the kitchen.

On the counter by the sink was a pale yellow Post-it; I steeled myself.

Hope you're OK. Speak later.

I looked at his plate, his knife, his coffee mug. I pressed my finger into the singed toast crumbs. When I licked it, there was a trace of marmalade. Did the note mean I could pretend the last thirty-six hours hadn't happened?

The kitchen window faced the terrace of shops across the road: a fried chicken shop, a solicitor's, and a launderette. Did I need to stop nights for the sake of me and Graham? Or look for another room to rent? Or was it worse? Did I need to start over in Taiwan? As a child, when I'd done wrong, I'd distract myself from the consequences with plans for escape: I'd imagine hitching to Durban, then stowing away on a ship . . .

As I was awash with fret, every option seemed acceptable, except not knowing. I dialed Graham's number.

"How're you feeling?" His voice was as detached as his Post-it.

"Not bad," I lied. "And you?"

"Anti-puke pills in the cabinet."

"Thanks, Gray."

"Clothes in the wash."

"Thanks." Swallowing my shame, I focused on the solicitor's sign. "I'm sorry about yesterday. I had mezcal on an empty stomach and thought I'd be sociable for a change. Then it escalated—"

"I can't talk now."

"When I think of you waiting at my place—"

"Got to go, Meggie."

The solicitor's said J & B BLAC SON. PI KING P THE PIEC S.

"Please, Graham. How can I make up?"

He was quiet.

Then he said, "It's not your fault you're my weakness."

"You're my weakness too," I said.

He groaned. "Urghhh, bye."

The phone cut off.

Urghhh, bye? I snorted my diva tears back. I had no diva rights. I had no rights. I didn't even deserve his acetaminophen.

Harnessing the energy of my guilt, I put on a pair of large yellow rubber gloves and did the washing-up. I didn't stop there. I emptied the kitchen cupboards. Mopped the floors. Scrubbed. Vacuumed.

After defrosting the fridge, I disposed of everything past its expiry date. But for all my efforts, I felt no better. As parts of the previous day seeped back into memory, my relief at Graham's not having broken up with me was replaced by a less comforting cycle of thoughts.

What have I done? I can't move in with him. Can't move in with someone I talk about like that. I've messed this up. I don't want to hurt him. How do I get out of it? What have I done? And why, on the day of my move, did I kiss Sabine?

Once the flat was so spick-and-span it would have impressed my mother, I lay down shaky and sweaty on the kitchen floor. My phone next to me on the linoleum tiles vibrated with a text.

Sabine: *you ok*

I didn't want to reply. Didn't want to see her, or anyone else from nights, ever again. Perhaps it *was* time to move, not just home, but country. Give up the booze. Do something good. Sign up with VSO like the real lesbian, the Swedish one, had.

But my renegade thumb typed: *Cool—you?*

Sabine: *cool too*

I turned the Nokia's screen facedown. But the six-word conversation revived me enough to topple a Sunny Delight from the fridge shelf. I sucked at the fake juice until the bottle conked in for a gasp. When my phone beeped again, I skimmed it across the tiles, out of reach.

Then I crawled over the floor to fetch it.

Sabine: *want me to come round*

Me (leaving off the punctuation and caps like she did): *im at grahams*

Sabine: *i know we shared a taxi remember*

I didn't remember. Me: *yes ok come*

I reread the sequence of messages. One moment I was full of regret, the next I was being an idiot again.

Yet, humming a Jacques Brel tune while I splashed my armpits with cologne from a dusty bottle in Graham's cupboard, I couldn't deny: the spirit of the day had lifted.

Opening the door to Sabine, my awe of her was for a moment too much. Her skin glowed, her hair was glossy; her limbs, though slim, were curved with muscle. I wondered if us having sex would be an antidote, if it would defuse things as it had with the Swedish woman.

Then I noticed how much she'd girlied up. Under her duffel coat, she wore a skimpy yellow dress and black ankle boots. She had pink pearl polish on her minute nails and a dusting of eyeshadow, lipstick, blush. I interpreted it as a retraction from dykey inclinations. Or could it be to impress my boyfriend, since we were at his flat?

Leading the way to the kitchen, I felt like my teenage self again, bell-shaped and stale. I needed a drink. A couple of beer cans knocked against the fridge door. On the top shelf, the Winston Churchill lay prominent in its box.

"Fan-cy," said Sabine in her soft, low drawl behind me.

"Need more than fancy on my side later," I said.

I passed a can to Sabine but she shook her head. "No beer?"

She wrinkled her nose.

I put her can back and tapped the top of mine but didn't open it. "Graham's upset with me."

"S'understandable."

"I know."

She hitched herself up onto the counter by the sink. *I'll break up with him! Today! Mark my word!*

"Sabine. Please don't—"

"And later? He rang and rang. We all said, Meggie, answer! But you didn't want—"

"I'm an arse," I said. "Can't stay with someone I treat like that."

"*He* doesn't know."

"But *I* know," I said, my face hot. "And everybody else knows."

She swung her legs back and forth. Then leaning over the sink, she opened the tap and drank. I pictured Graham's slight frown. She wiped her wet lips with the back of her hand. The rim of the tap was smudged with lipstick.

I should offer her a glass, I thought. But I didn't want to be the kind of person who offered glasses, who insisted on doing things the conventional way.

Taking the Winston Churchill from the fridge, I opened its velvet-lined box. I slit the foil, unpeeled it, and popped the cork to release a small genie of vapor. In a tribute to her ways, I took a swig from the neck.

My mouth filled with bubbles; I choked.

Laughing, she whacked my back. "Can tell you don't have French blood!"

While I continued to cough, she moved efficiently around the kitchen. She found the long-stemmed *poshies* at the back of the Tupperware shelf in no time. She took the champagne from me, stood the glasses side by side, and filled them up.

I'd always liked Graham's front room. Once, when he was at football practice, I spent an entire afternoon lying on his leather sofa watching the breeze in the leaves of a conker tree. But the tree had been hacked back at the start of winter, and as I sat on the sofa with Sabine, the room, rather than feeling peacefully spare, felt sparse.

She leaned over the sofa arm to the console and fingered through Graham's CDs. They were all either jazz or classical. She chose Prokofiev's *Romeo and Juliet*.

"My favorite ballet," I said.

"You like ballet?"

"When I was a kid I wanted to be a dancer. I was crap at it. But I couldn't stop reading those fifties books: *A Dream of Sadler's Wells, Veronica at the Wells, Masquerade at the Wells, No Castanets at the Wells* . . ."

Sabine bobbed her head to the violins' soaring opening.

Embarrassed, I pressed eject. "What have you got in your bag?"

From the discs in her flipcase, I selected a CD she'd been handed at a club night called TrailerTrash. As soon as we put it on, the early afternoon atmosphere of the flat changed. We played it loudly while we talked and drank.

Above the TV, a tarnished seventies mirror was screwed into the wall. I kept gazing at our reflections. Then Sabine waved at me.

"It's the tint," I said. "Makes it look like we're in a fairy tale."

"Fairy-tale friends, no?"

I wanted to secrete myself away with her words, keep playing them over. But forcing my eyes from the mirror, I poured the last of the champagne. "Why d'you change your name to SJ?"

"If you always do everything the same, your brain gets in a rut."

"I've heard about brushing your teeth with your other hand. Or altering your route to work."

My phone beeped.

Graham: *Got a leaving do. Back by eight.*

"Your boyfriend?" said Sabine.

"Yes."

She ejected the TrailerTrash disc.

"Don't go. It's only two o'clock."

"Bathroom first," she said.

The moment Sabine left the room, the mirror emptied itself of the desirable life it had reflected. Alone, my face changed: I saw its asymmetry, its uneven texture. I saw the look of resignation; I was too young for such a look. I didn't want to be this person, or live in this flat, or even wait here until eight.

Taking the empty champagne bottle through to the kitchen, I dumped it in the bin. About to put our glasses in the sink, I noticed the smudge of red at the tap's rim. I listened to make sure Sabine was still at the other end of the flat. Then I put my mouth to the tap. I put my lips around where hers had been. I turned it on and drank as she had.

When I pulled back, her smudge was gone.

I went to fetch my denim bag from Graham's bedroom. I puffed his white pillows and smoothed his white duvet. Glancing at the glass of water on the bedside table, I felt bad. Then I smelled Sabine's scent.

I turned to her. "Fancy going out somewhere?"

"We can get the bus to Camden."

"Let's go," I said.

22

The pub roof garden was gaily decorated with what looked like giant cocktail umbrellas. Silk flowers corkscrewed the iron railing. The concrete tables were decorated with shells and a ragdoll in sunglasses lazed back with her pudgy cloth feet resting on one of them. Otherwise, unsurprisingly for a Tuesday afternoon in spring, we were the rooftop's only occupants.

Screwing up her eyes at the feeble sun, Sabine said, "So you didn't break up with Graham?"

I chewed the straw of my caipirinha. "It's more complicated than I made out."

"You're pregnant?"

"Not as complicated as that."

"What, then?" She took a cigarette from a crushed pack of menthols.

"I was supposed to move in with him. Yesterday."

She laughed. "Already you fucked up."

"Thanks, Sabine."

She fished in her rucksack for her skull lighter. "But, come. If you change your mind, it's better now, no?"

"You mean for Graham?"

"For both."

She was right; he'd find someone else. I foresaw a leggy woman in a floral dress: good-natured, pretty. Both successful lawyers, they shared sandwiches in lunch breaks at court. I put my head in my hands. My own future was less clear. "I've given notice on my room. I'll need to get another place."

The cigarette pack shot between my elbows. "We'll get a place."

"We?" The pack was empty.

"It makes sense." She lit up.

I said, "We're both night owls."

She gave her cockeyed smile. "*Deux chouettes.*"

Finishing off my caipirinha, I couldn't quite believe it.

I smiled back. "I'll get us more drinks to celebrate."

Someone had scrawled on the toilet door: *I'll call you Laurie. When you call me. And you can call me Al.* I took my mobile from my bag. The battery icon on the screen was flashing; it was days since I'd charged it. Before Graham's number could ring, the phone cut out. I pressed down hard on the power button. Dead.

A sign, said my more cautious voice. *You can't end your relationship like this.*

But another voice said, *It's going to be awful however you do it. You might as well get it over with.*

Not wanting to be a *mañana mañana* person, a Sherry

type, I slipped out of the pub. A bright red phone box stood like an exclamation mark at the bottom of the block.

I've always been amazed by how quickly things can change. One moment, I was swimming along about to embark on a cohabitation that might have led to a life together. If I'd kept going with the flow, perhaps there'd have been kids, grandkids, chromosomes forever entwined . . . Except the next I was clutching a bone-shaped piece of plastic in a urine-scented cubicle saying, "We need to break up."

"You're pissed again, Meggie?"

"It's not because of that."

"Where are you?"

"Call box."

"Look, we'll talk later."

"Graham, there's no point." A death rattle of coins went through. "I'm sorry, this is a crap way to do things."

"Actually, it's pretty fitting."

"If it's not going to work, it's better now—"

"Fuck off, Megan."

The line went so quiet I thought it was dead. "Graham?"

"I've one last thing to say to you."

I waited.

"You're obsessed with that woman. I don't know what she's like. But I feel sorry for her. It's terrible to be used like that."

I was stunned.

"As for you," he continued. "With her in your life, nothing's going to work out. No relationships. No literature studies. Nothing."

A long tone sounded. Then the automated voice: "The caller has hung up. Please replace the handset. The caller has hung—"

I wanted to howl down the line. He'd got it so wrong.

Failing at law school, I'd expected to die of shame. But after my mother said, *You're no child of mine*, all I felt was relief. Coming to the UK was about escape. But once I was here, I didn't know how to be different. Didn't have the imagination, didn't have the guts. And if we lived together, if it went well, aged fifty I might still feel that way . . .

"The caller has hung up," repeated the automated voice.

A bleary-eyed woman was banging on the door.

I slammed the handset pointlessly into the bracket and went back to the pub.

Waiting for a pack of menthols and a couple of gold-flaked tequilas at the bar, I resolved not to mention what I'd done to Sabine. It would be better to keep things separate in my mind. Besides, I didn't want to spoil this day, which, while marking the end of me and Graham Willoughby, meant something entirely different for me and Sabine Dubreil.

After we'd knocked our tequilas back, I said, "Know what, SJ? I'm also going to change my name."

"What's your middle one?"

"Greta. Yours?"

"Don't have." She flicked her cigarette into a potted plant. "MG is magnesium."

"How d'you know that?"

"I did chemistry at school. Of metals, MG has the lowest melting point."

"Not cool like SJ, then?"

She lifted her rucksack onto the table. "If you really want change, it's best to start small."

I put my paperback-sized bag alongside hers.

"No." Shaking her head, she opened the drawstring. "You need a sack like mine. With this one, you can go anywhere, do anything." She turned the rucksack upside down. "Look."

I gazed at the things of her life, freely displayed before me: Guerlain Shalimar perfume, asthma inhaler, skull lighter, makeup, condoms, boxer knickers, frilly knickers, tights, the flipbook of CDs, Walkman, tissues, a hand-knitted chicken, toothpaste, toothbrush, a slim silver wallet, a broken compact mirror, mint gum, a fold-up hairbrush, and a passport.

"A passport?" I said.

"I'm portable," she said. "We both need to be portable. Let's find you a rucksack too."

In Camden Market, I withdrew the last of my overdraft from a machine that charged. Egged on by Sabine, I bought a yellow rucksack printed with sunflowers. I transferred the meager contents of my bag (lip gloss, earphones, Walkman, phone, Jean Rhys novel, coin purse), then splurged on whatever took our fancy. Two lipsticks labeled Toffee Apple that Sabine said were classic Marilyn. Two vintage compact mirrors with Victoriana cases. Giant slices of doughy pizza. Paper cups of overpriced sangria. A yellow silk scarf (for Sabine) and a flowing sea-green dress (Sabine's idea, for me). At the slightest hesitation in our spree, I'd say, "What next?" Then she'd suggest something, and we'd do it.

Only when the stalls began to pack up did we stop. I thought we'd reached the end of our adventure. But a few blocks on, Sabine pulled me into a basement lined with plants in glass cases. Specifically, cacti and mushrooms. I'd always envied how people talked of psychedelic trips. Sabine asked the rainbow-haired assistant to see a box of fine shrooms with narrow stems and floaty heads.

"What d'you think?" she said.

"Let's get them," I said.

"Twenty-five quid a box," said the assistant.

"One, please," said Sabine, and I coughed up.

A couple of hours after we'd eaten the shrooms, Camden Town transformed into an early evening parade of storybook characters. People pretending to be shop assistants, bus drivers, metalheads, rock chicks. I hadn't expected the trip to be this palpably material. The sky was a blue so smooth it seemed like we were inside a balloon. Around us, the parade was moving to the thrum of the earth turning. I could hear the thrum, every hollow in my body filled with its vibrations.

I was about to ask Sabine if she could feel it too when she said, "Fuck, I must get to the airport."

I started to laugh, then couldn't stop. She caught the giggle bug from me and couldn't stop either. We sat on the cracked pavement, cheeks cramping, bellies aching. She kept trying to gain control, to speak again, but the battle on her face was even funnier than her words. Finally, she dragged me to a vendor selling freshly squeezed orange juice. I signaled to him for two cups. We gulped them down.

"Juice neutralizes shrooms," she said.

I bought two more, which we drank less desperately.

Then she said, "I must fly to Hong Kong to join Lucian."

My urge to laugh stalled. I thought, *Who's Lucian?* Then I thought, *I'd better not ask.* She'd probably already told me. Then I asked anyway, "Who's Lucian?"

"A crime writer," she said, biting at a nail. "Nobody here's heard of him but he's big in, I don't know, Japan and the rest of the world. He's got a wife and kids but travels a lot. I travel with him."

The way she said it, I knew she hadn't told me. I felt my face go dark. I saw myself as a pathetic conquest: her plaything, her paying thing.

"You're going to fly while you're high?" I no longer felt very high myself.

She started to laugh again while waving for a black cab. "We'll share. I'm going home first."

In my newfound semi-sobriety, I drew the line. I wouldn't

pay for a taxi so she could go back and pack her things. "I'm not going home."

The cab pulled up; she opened the door.

"What about getting a flat?" I asked.

She flitted her hand through the air. "I'll SMS."

As we hugged goodbye, she whispered, "Wish I was going to Hong Kong with you."

Yeah, I thought, *sure you do. Me and my open purse.*

All I said was, "*Ciao*, hey. Have fun."

23

Over the next fortnight, I got no messages from Sabine.

Luckily, my landlady said I could postpone moving out. In anger at my general foolishness, I lived more punitively than ever. The resolve was helped by being broke. I had basic foodstuffs in my cupboard but no money for anything else. I saw no one and, other than my scheduled runs, went nowhere. Days I spent trying to sleep, nights trying to study, but failed dismally at both. The only thing I managed with any success was to block out thoughts about Graham; guilt at how I'd treated him made it easy.

Determined to move on, I took stock of where I was. I'd been in the UK for over two years, in London for over one, doing nights for almost five months. I hadn't found my niche but shift work provided the time to do so. If I stayed nocturnal a bit longer I'd surely get used to it. If I hoped to one day find a job linked to books, I was doing the right degree. Finishing with Graham meant losing his social circle but I'd cope. As an only child, I was used to my own company.

With renewed dedication to my studies, I tried to accept my solitary, marginal life. But it didn't happen. Instead, I began to crave aspects of the ordinary I'd never craved before. Light, noise, color, people. One night, I blew out my black candles, shut down my computer, and walked four miles to a 24/7 supermarket.

I'd always had an aversion to supermarkets. They epitomized domesticity, suburbia, the life I didn't want to have. But that night! Light, noise, color, people, life! I wandered up and down the broad aisles, smiling at the packers, making meaningless chitchat, looking in wonder at the jaunty yellow cereal boxes, the cheerful cows on the cheese wedges, the heavy, globular avocados, the smiling bunches of bananas, the little fly that had come in from the outside world to buzz over some spilt blueberry yogurt on the floor; the marvelous, enviable little fly that tomorrow would return to the sunshiny, bustling, ordinary, everyday outside world.

The experience reminded me of the mushrooms at their most fun with Sabine. I didn't want to leave; I stayed in the supermarket until dawn. When the sun came up over the car park and whited out the night, I stood there on the empty tarmac staring into the bright, brilliant light.

Nocturnality wasn't working. I needed a new plan. But my

numbed-out brain couldn't come up with one. Reluctantly I walked home, I ate my pasta, I lay in bed.

Then the next shift began.

24

While my mind shut off every avenue leading to Graham, it was more capricious with Sabine.

At first, I did everything I could not to bump into her. I came in early, left late, and avoided the lavatories on the corridor where I'd first seen her. I didn't talk to anyone more than was absolutely necessary. It was easy since at the start of shift everyone else was in their own world too.

But as the mood of the week lifted, my annoyance diminished. I became curious. Then, I became careless. And then, the pendulum swung the other way. I'd arrive on time, pause by the Energy door, use the lavatory that both teams used, and go more than I needed. I'd hang around by the photocopier and loiter on the Energy floor. Once, I even found an excuse to wander into Energy's offices—but there was no sign of her.

Stumped, I couldn't ask anyone where she was because *we* were supposed to be friends. Close friends, even. Lovers, some might have assumed.

What a joke.

Maybe if I got to know her better we could be one or all of those things. As it was, I didn't even know what continent she was on. Quite likely, she and Lucian had decided to stay in Hong Kong.

No sooner had I resigned myself to the idea than in my pigeonhole I found a surprise.

Behind my usual hefty stack of newspapers was a blank white envelope, not sealed or even folded closed. It contained a single stalls ticket to *Romeo and Juliet* at the Royal Opera House the next night, Friday night, before work.

The rest of the shift passed in a blur of distracted thinking. Sabine hadn't left the country. She hadn't abandoned the friendship. She hadn't been using me for money. Perhaps she'd lost her phone, or forgotten about messaging me. Or, perhaps I shouldn't make excuses for her. She played games, she was unreliable—but that was her nature. The counterbalance was excitement, spontaneity. As for living together, that had been a bad idea. Had I ever truly wanted it? I needed to stop getting pissed off about things I didn't want. The gifts were special; didn't they show that I was special to her? The thing was not to ever count on Sabine. What was so great about reliability after all? Wasn't it enough that she was special to me too?

At home, I tried on the sea-green dress I'd thought I'd never wear. It looked better than anything I'd have chosen for myself. I needed elegant shoes to match; supermarket sneakers would hardly do. In a local charity shop, I found a pair of high silver slingbacks. I spent the afternoon walking around in them. With the house to myself, I played Jacques Brel full blast. I sauntered about my bedroom, then the sitting room, then down the stairs to make a coffee in the kitchen.

Through the ceiling, I heard the high electronic vibration behind Brel's plea. *Ne me quitte pas, Ne me quitte pas, Ne me quitte pas, Ne me quitte pas.*

25

Light reflected off the Royal Opera House's golden curlicue; it shimmered in the crystal chandeliers.

Sabine hadn't said where to meet and I didn't want to spoil the magic of her ticket with a humdrum text. The red carpet was sumptuous beneath my heels as I crossed the foyer scouring the women. Some wore evening gowns and jewels; some were such balletomanes that their outfits resembled ballerina-type garb.

The auditorium bell rang. Presumably, Sabine expected us to meet at our seats. When I found the right entrance, I joined the queue in front of it. I pictured the dancers standing in the wings: clavicles vibrating with their heartbeats, bodies alert. I felt like I was in the wings too. Soon I would be next to Sabine.

A striking couple stood near a recess a little way through the crowd. The woman had a long back exposed in a low-slung silk dress. Her black hair was fixed into some kind of knot with a tortoiseshell comb. The man appeared to be much older: tall, debonair, with notably thick, gray locks. I assumed he was her father until I saw him put his hand on the exposed skin of her lower back. The whole of his hand, the flat of his palm. He slid it down, beneath the draping of the top, to the very base of her spine. It seemed wrong but I couldn't look away. I felt aroused at what he was doing, as if his hand were there on the base of my spine, holding it, cupping it. The woman arched her back into him, then slipped from his hold and turned.

It was Sabine.

The ticket wasn't intended for me. The envelope hadn't had my name on it. What had made me assume it was mine? Sabine had left it in my pigeonhole by mistake. I had to leave; I stepped out of the queue.

Sabine saw me.

Too late.

But her face lit up. Her lips parted; her eyes crinkled. She rushed over and grabbed my hands. "I *knew* you'd be so beautiful in the dress!"

"I didn't recognize you," I said. "Your hair's . . . grown?"

"Trick comb." She tucked back a loose curl. The tall, gray-haired man had joined us. "Lucian, meet Meggie."

He opened his arms. The lining of his jacket was smoky patterned silk; his white shirt was textured with white embroidery. He smelled of frankincense cut with a trace of cigar. He held the hug he gave me for a fraction too long.

Breaking away, I asked, "How was Hong Kong?"

Lucian raised his eyebrows to Sabine.

"Tokyo," she said. "We stayed in a glass hotel with a bar you'd love. Views in every direction. A man played a white piano around the clock."

"Not the same man, of course," said Lucian.

"No," said Sabine, "in shifts, like us."

Before anyone could ask about my time off, the highlight of which had been a visit to an around-the-clock supermarket, the auditorium bell sounded its final call.

I was following Sabine towards our row when Lucian pushed in front of me. On reaching our seats, he sat down between the two of us. I assumed she'd swap places when she noticed. But while the orchestra tuned up, she simply reached across his lap to take my hand.

Lucian leaned back with a closet smile as Sabine drew my fingers to her lips. She'd made this gesture before. But now I saw his hand move between her legs. The tendons rose under his skin as he pressed. Were there expectations for the evening that I hadn't realized? The lights dimmed; the auditorium was quiet. Then Sabine bit the tip of my finger. I cried out.

"Shhhh," someone said.

A twitch of amusement passed between the two of them.

*

While Sabine watched the ballet, Lucian watched her. Sometimes she whispered to him; sometimes I caught him glancing at me. In different circumstances, his attention might have made me feel good. But here, everything was related to their sexual dynamic. When the curtains came down after the passionate balcony scene, I told them I had to make a call.

Around the corner in Floral Street, I bummed a cigarette from a sulky teenager in a suit. Then I leaned against the wall by the bins, smoking. My money was on the ballet being Sabine's suggestion but Lucian's funds, Sabine's friend but Lucian's fantasy. What was his fantasy, though?

I didn't need to go back, I told myself, crushing the cigarette under my shoe.

But during the second act, watching the playful carnival dances, my perspective shifted. Perhaps I was being curmudgeonly. If Lucian and Sabine were a bit silly, a bit insensitive, they were also lustily in love. If having a witness to their liaison heightened it, was that so terrible?

When the lights went up for the interval, Sabine hooked her arm through mine, "so you don't disappear again," and suggested some champagne. She steered us up the carpeted stairs to the newly renovated Floral Hall.

The room was spectacular: glass and ironwork and light and mirrors. It had a barrel-roofed Victorian atrium with tall tables and bar stools shaped like plants.

"Where's Lucian?" I asked.

"Calling his wife."

"Do you mind that he's married?"

"No," she said, "I like it."

"Why?"

"We don't have the sort of thing that goes with domestic life."

Waiting at one of the tables, I watched Sabine move towards a bar with sculpted metal leaves. I wondered what kind of thing she and Lucian had, exactly. In my relationships, age had been incidental. But with Sabine and Lucian, the gap of thirty-odd years seemed integral. He was an older man who clearly adored his younger woman; what was it like to be adored like that? Protected, cherished, as a father might cherish his little girl.

Sabine brought back a bottle and two wide-brimmed glasses.

While I poured, she slipped a finger under the neckline of her dress. Hooking a silver choker, she moved its pendant to the front.

I stared. "That's stunning."

"I guess it's part of me." She shrugged. "My fate."

The Alexander McQueen scarab glistened against her pale, slender neck.

"Graham once gave me a sheep," I said. "I forgot it at his flat. So I guess it wasn't my fate."

She gave a puzzled smile.

"Lucian's not the kind of guy who'd give you a sheep," I said.

"No."

"I mean, a sheep jewel."

She touched it, frowning. "Lucian didn't give me the beetle."

I held a mouthful of champagne against my palate until the bubbles went flat. Then I swallowed. "Who did?"

She kept rubbing the back of her pendant as if exploring it. I knew the words engraved there.

"Was it . . . another lover?" I prodded.

"That's one way to put it," she said softly.

I poured more champagne. She drank hers as if it was lemonade, so I did the same. Then I filled our glasses again.

"D'you know," she said, "I was going to be a dancer once."

"Like me?"

"Did the training. Look."

She shifted her legs at the ankle. She nudged off one black heel then the other and pointed her stockinged feet. I was surprised at the enviably high arches, the deep curves. She slid off her stool and stood on her tiptoes. She lifted one foot to the knee with perfect turnout, perfect balance. Holding the table lightly like a barre, she moved en pointe.

"Stop," I said, wincing. "Without shoes you'll hurt yourself."

"My feet are already fucked." She rested her weight back against her stool. "That's why I couldn't go on." What she'd done would have been painful but it seemed to cheer her up.

"When I was small, I collected ballet programs," I said. "I kept track of the dancers as they rose through the ranks. My mother thought I was peculiar—"

"You were a serious child." She looked at me with affection.

115

Then she said, "My parents didn't have money. We didn't go to the theater, these sorts of things. But my brother took me to see ballet films in the town hall every Sunday night."

"Your brother?" She'd never mentioned siblings before. I'd assumed she was an only child like me.

The auditorium bell rang.

I wanted to ask her more but I'd pried too much.

She slipped her feet back into her shoes. We gulped the last of our drinks and returned to our seats.

For the third act, it was a relief not to be next to Sabine. I needed space to think about what she'd said. She was someone who had a brother, who'd loved ballet enough to train to be a dancer, who'd been doing what I dreamed of even before I knew her. But also, there was the thing about the "lover" who'd given her the scarab. What did she mean by it?

At Juliet's bedside scene, I reimagined Sabine as the ballerina. I watched Juliet trying to wake Romeo, shaking his lifeless body, putting his limp arms around her. Lucian slipped an arm around Sabine. I saw him watching her solicitously in the dark, his cherished little girl. Suddenly, I had a profound ache of confused envy. I didn't want to hold Sabine myself; I wanted to be held like that.

Juliet used her last moment to reach out for Romeo's hand. Then their families came in to find them, fingers entwined.

After the crimson-and-gold house curtains fell, we followed the dazed audience into the street. Lucian summoned a black cab.

He looked at Sabine, and then to me, and then back to Sabine.

She shook her head.

"Shame." From the cab, he blew us kisses. Lowering the window, he called, "Thanks, Sabine, for the stupendous treat!"

Sabine's treat? As we headed towards the Thames, I did the maths. Altogether, the tickets would have cost a month's rent. How could Sabine afford that? I'd thought the ballet was her idea. But had she also been the instigator of some sexual fantasy?

It started to rain lightly, rain like damp lace. Then the rain became heavier. We hurried along in melancholic silence with our heads bowed. I was sure it was my fault. Because I hadn't contributed to the intended spirit of the evening. Because I'd pressed her to open up, to speak of things that were hard.

I said, "Let's find a cashpoint."

"Now?"

"I owe you, Sabine."

She was annoyed. "I don't want your money."

I kept my eyes focused ahead. She didn't want anything particular from me, nor for me to do anything I didn't want to do. By Southwark Bridge, I spotted a pub with a stained-glass door. Friday night glowed promisingly through it. I hooked my arm in hers, as she had mine earlier. "I'm getting you a drink at least."

Several tequilas later, the rain had subsided. Although we hadn't spoken of anything much, our mood had shifted to become dreamy and close. As we crossed over to the other side of the river, I thought of how I'd almost left the theater, almost ended everything before it had even begun. I resolved not to let it happen again. I wanted whatever we had, whatever we might have, at any cost.

The lights beside the water plated the Thames silver and gold. With lemon and salt still tanging my lips, I felt exhilarated. What Sabine had said at Graham's when she saw us in the tarnished mirror was coming true. *Fairy-tale friends.*

PART IV

26

From the moment I gave in to my craving for her, everything changed. Sabine was no longer a catalyst for what I wanted, she was it. I longed to know her, to know about her—but more than that, to *be* her. Tired of the rooms in my own dreary house, done with measly alterations, I let go, the house burned down . . . and it felt good.

Though Sabine set the terms of our togetherness, I accepted them. In part, her unreliable ways were the flip side to her playful qualities. In part her talk, especially at the ballet and in Valentines, had hinted at a past that deserved allowances. But mostly, her influence gave me permission to explore a freer version of myself.

I lost touch with old friends; what we used to discuss came to seem dull, our bonds circumstantial. Phone calls to my mother, never regular, became rare. I took to using international cards in call boxes. It was easier to steer away from her despair in a public place, on a handset greasy with others' fingerprints.

Since Sabine wasn't solely nocturnal, I stopped trying to be that too. Shifts on, I was; shifts off, I wasn't. My brain felt constantly woolly but it no longer seemed necessary to be sharp. Mainly this was because I'd quit my literature studies. If I did it with some regret, I reassured myself the decision was temporary. The longer I stayed away from my books, the surer I felt.

As an outsider, I'd always found refuge in reading. But as Sabine and I grew closer, I didn't need it. My outsider's life began to feel extraordinary. I didn't want to read about characters, I wanted to be them. I didn't want to read about adventures, I wanted to have them.

Sabine made our lives feel like enough of a story in itself.

After the night at the Royal Opera House, nine months since Sabine and I had first met, our friendship accelerated. No longer stuck in the house of the self, I felt as if I was on a long journey in a sleeper train with a changeling companion. A train that sped through unknown territory, not stopping at timetabled stations but arbitrarily here and there.

With late spring as good a time for change as any, I moved into the small flat in New Cross that Earl shared with his dog, Coño. It was an easygoing environment: relaxed and sociable with a regular flux of guests when Earl was around. Although Sabine and I never spoke of living together again, she enjoyed rocking up there with her rucksack full of food. She'd cook for us, and whoever else, a meal that was hearty and homely.

"Meatballs in fruit sauce served on mash, Meggie, Earl?"

"*Soupe à l'oignon* with fat slices of crusty bread?"

"Boozy mussels fresh today from Borough Market? *Quatre, cinq, six?*"

She prepared the food conscientiously like a *maman* but ate voraciously, greedily, like a teenage boy.

The few times she stayed over, she slept on my mattress in a tank top and panties. After falling asleep, she'd kick the duvet off. By day she tended to be cold, particularly her hands and feet; by night she was always hot. Occasionally I'd lie like a succubus with my gaze fixed on whatever part of her was in view: an elbow with the shadow of a bruise on it or the oval soap curve of a breast pressed into a pillow. More often, though, I kept my eyes screwed closed since it was in bed I felt most estranged from her. We never cuddled or held hands or let so much as a foot touch a foot. It was as if she regarded the bed solely for sleep, and sleep a solemnly private matter.

Being so close to her yet so far, I would get a strange sensation in my belly. She was there, she wasn't there; she was by my side but I couldn't reach her.

Obsession is about not wanting to be the self. Wanting to be *other*. Next to her, I must have known, at some level, the ultimate impossibility of that.

When it came to kissing, Sabine and I did it only drunk and in public. Sometimes, I enjoyed the performance; surfing her wave of exhibitionism could be fun. Other times, it irritated me, though not entirely without contrariety . . .

Coming from a starchy, puritanical environment, I rejected pointless sexual boundaries. The more I knew of Sabine, the more I wanted to know. And I wanted to be wanted, of course. But I was also ambivalent about us getting more physical. Sex involves expression; fascination allows negation. My confused feelings were tossed about by our pushes and pulls, by frustration, curiosity, and pride.

The closest we came to discussing it was at the Ladies' Pond in Hampstead. I recall the texture of the day clearly. Trying to lick the Smarties off before the soft-serve melted as we crossed the road to the Heath. My mouth filled with the sickly mix of chocolate, strawberry, and caramel as we wandered along the paths through the trees. My fingers still sticky when we sat on the cement at the edge of the cold, broad pool.

Spontaneously, Sabine had suggested we go swimming. We were wearing lost property bathing suits that the lifeguard, charmed by her, had found us. For hygiene's sake, we'd put them on inside out; they were too big and slightly damp. Sabine's was tan with crisscross straps. Mine was pink with white dots and had a residual scent of coconut oil.

When the sun shone the afternoon felt almost summery, but it kept disappearing. As the cement flickered from cream to gray, I traced a crack with a long stick of grass. The water under my feet was clean but not clear; almost golden at the surface, though smoky mustard deeper down. The air was so quiet I could hear the crackle of a dragonfly's wings.

Then Sabine said, "I leave every person I fuck."

"You've never been left?"

"Not once."

"You're too proud, Sabine!"

She swung her pale muscled legs back and forth, toes skimming the water without splashing. "Do you ever imagine us having sex?"

"Sometimes," I said. "Do you?"

"Sometimes."

I flung the trembling stick of grass away.

"An Austrian director told me actors often want to do it with each other," she said. "They want to do it badly. And it's great for the film. It keeps the, what d'you call . . ."

"Tension?"

"No, electricity. It keeps the electricity between them strong. But sometimes, the actors get weak. They give in. And then"—she blew the air out between her lips—"*pfff.*"

"*Pfff?*" I said.

"If you watch, you can see the exact moment. This scene, this scene: exciting. Then, *pfff.*"

I had a deflated moment of my own. "You agree with him?"

She shrugged.

"You think fucking is weak?" I said.

"What if it is?"

"What are you, a nun?" I hugged my knees tight to my chest.

Her back straightened, eyes cut. "What if I like it weak?

What if I like it dirty, fucked up? What if I like it pushed to where you don't even exist—"

"I like that too."

"But, Meggie, if we went there, you and I, we'd never come back. We'd skid off the piste, lose everything. We'd eat each other alive, cannibalize each other."

I gazed at the silky gusset of my loaned costume. "After we were done, I'd dump you so as not to be like all the others you've left."

She gave a hurt laugh.

Was this our moment that I'd ruined?

I put an arm across her narrow shoulders. She picked at my costume straps. She flicked them against my skin. Her cold hand pressed below my shoulder blades. I felt her cold palm on the other side of my heart.

She pushed.

I fell forwards, headlong into the pond.

Surfacing from the icy water, I gasped, choking. Sabine pin-dropped in beside me and pulled me under. We wrestled. I couldn't see a thing but I had her in my grasp. I held on to her. In the privacy of the murk, I didn't disguise my obvious determination. Then abruptly her face appeared in front of mine, so close it almost touched. I rearranged my features; she didn't. I held her longer than I should have.

Above the water, she spat a stream into my eyes. We raced to the other side and I let her beat me to it. After circling the pond a few times, we floated together into the middle.

The sun was a dazzling pom-pom that whitened out the sky. I wanted to store what I saw as a bright mental photograph.

But what has stayed with me instead is the image of Sabine when she appeared up close. Her expression as I held on to her was not spirited, as I might have expected, or determined, or even angry. Her eyes were blank, her jaw was slack; her face was vacant.

27

Just as in company Sabine and I kissed whereas on our own we didn't, in company we talked a lot about sex. *Yes, you can be a feminist and a sex worker. Yes, being a dominatrix is a bit like being a therapist. Yes, exploring destructive fantasies in sexual play can be empowering.* We did it with the other nightshifters, as well as with complete strangers: people we met in pubs, on buses, in markets, and at clubs. They bought us drinks, gave us drugs; invitations fell like winnings into our laps.

One time in Camden Market we found a stall selling fetish furniture. I was in a green skirt with a tight purple dragon T-shirt. She was in a knitted minidress, navy with black stars. We wandered among heavily carved beds with ornate hook-and-eye headboards. Sabine ran her hand down a chair that looked like a throne with a hole in the seat. We made silly faces in the shadows cast by a spiky wrought-iron lamp. As we passed a bench contraption that resembled an inclined leg press, I slapped my palm on the cushion.

"Do you like my work?" A gaunt man with an emerald goatee and a double-angled nose emerged from a door at the back.

"Very cool," said Sabine.

"Looking for something special?"

"Just looking."

"How about this?" He showed us what appeared to be a collection of intricately decorated leather straps and silver buckles.

Sabine ran her fingers over them.

"My own design. You won't find it anywhere else." He spoke with a slight Polish accent. "You want to feel the weight?"

I held out my arms; it weighed more than I'd expected. "Hea-vy."

He quickly took it back. "But very comfortable. Want to try it on?"

Once he'd fastened the buckles to my wrists, torso, and ankles, I was wearing a swing. He yelled to a woman at the back who hurried over with a stepladder. He lifted me up and attached the harness to a scaffolding bar above our heads. A small crowd had gathered below us. He called to his assistant again and Górecki's *Symphony of Sorrowful Songs* swelled through the stall's speakers. He gave me a little push; I curved back and began to fly.

Though I knew the affecting music was based on words

etched into a wall by a Gestapo prisoner, I couldn't help being moved as I flew through the air in the erotic harness. Was it really less than a year since I'd been wearing a top with a cerise bow that my mother had chosen for me?

When I came down from the heights, the emerald-goateed man invited us to a castle in Germany. He organized a festival there every full moon. He said he'd be honored if we'd attend as his guests.

We never made it there; our only trip away together was to Eastbourne. But after listening in on the conversation, a woman with a diamanté mohawk told us about a club in east London called Studio X. She raved about the circus freaks theme so much that we decided to give it a go . . .

At the next blowout with our crew, Sabine was away with Lucian. The rest of us sat around a low table in a basement flat with the blinds pulled down. Candles in an assortment of stalagmited bottles were scattered here and there. Missing Sabine, I longed to conjure up the spirit of our times together. After a few snorts of crushed-up MDMA crystals, I told the crew of our find.

"Imagine a seedy, intimate club under a railway bridge," I said. "It's open every night of the week. Imagine cheap, generous drinks. Drugs available on request from the doorman too. Imagine comfy sofas, a space-age dance floor, and an ancient harem with a dungeon touch. A black club cat called Slinky making eyes at you."

"Sounds like a dream," Sherry sighed.

Encouraged, I carried on, "Imagine no look required, all looks accepted. Being as comfortable to chat the night away as to spend it in a dark room. Imagine a secret dock where the underworld of the city can wash up against anyone else. A true democracy of race, age, and gender—"

Prawn's pale, spotty face shone bright pink in the flickering light. "Dudess, you've got to fucking take us there!"

"When SJ's back," I said. "Promise."

28

Every time Sabine was away, she was incommunicado. It wasn't unusual; most of the crew had separate off-shift lives. Since she hardly touched her phone anyway, I supposed she got caught up in being wherever she was. Sometimes she forgot to say she was leaving but I accepted that too. She and Lucian often headed off at the last minute. Her disappearances didn't always correspond with her shifts but her opposite number seemed obliging. I assumed that he, a whippet-thin man with earnestly combed hair, was in love with her. It was easy to assume.

Although Sabine and I were more than merely work friends, I was proud that I didn't question her. That I didn't try to pin her down or make her conform to hackneyed etiquette. But I also had a more covert reason for my unpossessive attitude.

When we were together, I kept my obsession in check—but apart, I indulged it. Not that anybody would have guessed. I didn't talk about Sabine incessantly; I didn't talk about her at all. Instead, I discreetly tried to be as much like her as I could. The changes were subtle, hidden behind my skin. She was there in the way I held myself, the way my muscles arranged my face, the relaxation of my vocal cords into their softest, lowest drawl.

My external self, with what others had called its *teardrop* shape, *apricot-vanilla* coloring, and *friendly* accent, was contrary enough to Sabine's for the imitation to go unnoticed. But from the inside—unless I caught a glimpse of Meggie in a mirror, I could almost forget who I was.

The sensation was expansive; I felt newly wired, freshly connected to life. It happened with the crew, at Earl's parties, and with people Sabine didn't know. It happened with one-night stands before, during, and after sex. But it was the most intense when I indulged it alone.

Since I couldn't find clothes like Sabine's on Petticoat Lane, from charity shops I made up outfits similar in style. I hid them at the back of my wardrobe behind my jeans, sweaters, and camisoles. (Once I saw an astronomically priced designer jacket identical to hers; she told me she'd got her fake in Japan with Lucian for twenty quid. Japan was especially good for fakes, she said. The next time she went, she got me fake Vivienne Westwood gloves and I had to agree: indistinguishable from the real thing.)

Preparing to go out, I'd talk to myself using Sabine's cadences. I'd wash, dress, and apply makeup her way. Then I'd walk along the road with her gait. What I liked best, though, was to take on the version of Sabine that I'd never seen: the person I imagined she was by herself, for herself, when she was alone. I noticed what I thought she'd notice, went where I thought she'd go. I reacted in the way I thought she'd react when nobody was watching.

One weekday afternoon, I attended an exhibition of photographs by Francesca Woodman. Having selected it while channeling Sabine, I wandered around in the same vein. I paused at the self-portraits where she'd pause: the blur of a woman behind creased paper or the faceless woman curled towards a coiled eel in a bowl. I passed by the pictures whose titles alone would have made her yawn: *I'm Trying My Hand at Fashion Photography* or *It Must Be Time for Lunch, Now.*

Leaving the exhibition, I strolled on from the bars and buzz of the West End to the industrial buildings and new loft conversions of Clerkenwell. Segueing off to a lonely stretch of Regent's Canal, I saw a swan floating upside down on the water. Staring pensively, it took a while before I realized the bird was dead.

Hurrying away through the back streets of Islington, I came upon a French café. After taking a table under a kitsch mural of the Sacré-Coeur, I ordered a pastis, which I'd never ordered, or seen Sabine order, but could picture her doing in the circumstances. Sipping it slowly, I let my ears flood with "Sweet Dreams" off the Marilyn Manson album she'd burned for me.

29

Convinced that Sabine's sexual past was aligned with our wilder leanings, it bothered me that mine wasn't. To catch up, I decided to treat my body as something to be used, to use it to gain access to what was outside my usual realm.

Early on, I made the mistake of trying to explain this to Earl. On a walk with Coño to Peckham Common, I told him how sex gave you a shortcut into other people's lives. You got to meet a range of individuals more varied than you would by ordinary socializing.

"You mean sex with women?" Earl said.

I shrugged. "Mostly with men."

Earl grimaced. "Men are animals, Meggie."

"Women are animals too, Earl."

He shook his head. "It's not the same thing."

We waited for a van to reverse out in front of us.

"A guy might be getting what he wants," I said. "But I get what I want too."

"Which is?"

"Connection. After fucking, people tell you things you'd hear no other way. They open up to you. Like that, you're in their home, their bedroom, their fantasies—"

"You want to be careful whose fantasies you're in."

"But I don't! That's the whole point, Earl. I don't want to *curate* people according to what I think I like. Or *standards*. Or the need for mutual attraction even."

Earl was dismayed.

"I want to use my body to access all of it," I said. "Uncensored."

As we crossed over onto the Common, he said with real concern, "That's not *respecting* yourself, Meggie."

I was deeply annoyed with him then. Unhooking Coño's leash, I ran off with her across the grass. Why was it such a great thing to respect yourself? If you let go of vapid ideas like that, of that kind of preciousness, you could explore so much else. If you swept your precious self out of the way a bit.

After the conversation with Earl, I refrained from telling anybody quite how much I swept my own precious self aside. Often, I had to do it with a steel broom because it didn't come naturally. I'd research edgy encounters in clunky forums online; then, fueled with wine, I'd force myself into the field. Yet, years later, it's the incongruous intimacy with strangers that sticks in my mind more than the actual sex. Small, personal details . . . A smell like boiled sausages on the neck of a wealthy, well-groomed man. The to-do list on a young woman's fridge that ended with *BE KIND!* Erotic art books placed backwards on cluttered bookshelves. A dusty box of tampons in a man's otherwise meticulous bathroom.

For casual lovers, I had only four rules, though I treated them as gospel: I'd have sex drunk, but never on drugs; I'd have sex privately in public places (bathrooms or locked parks at night), but never publicly in clubs; I refused to have sex without condoms; and I never invited anyone back to Earl's. The last was important, not because of what Earl might think but because being away meant I could escape. I don't recall ever not wanting to escape as soon as the sun came up.

One morning I crept out of a Soho apartment before the guy I'd slept with was awake. Aside from a foam mattress, the place had been bare. He'd said it belonged to an old friend of his who was an artist. The luminous sign saying MODEL flashed above the building's open doorway as I left.

Sashaying through the streets of Covent Garden, I felt fine and carefree in my short yellow dress and black ankle boots. Soon I became aware of a man with a large camera behind me taking snaps. I kept walking but secretly I courted it. I flirted, he followed me; I paused outside a high-end lingerie shop that was just opening. He stopped a few paces back. In the plate glass, his hair was thick and white; his tanned cheeks had deep vertical creases.

Wandering around the shop's interior, I fingered a salmon lace negligee.

"You like it?" he said in a European accent I couldn't place.

I nodded.

He took it to the counter and paid for it, then asked if I wanted a bag.

I said, "No."

He gave me the parcel wrapped in black tissue paper and tied with golden string. We walked outside together. "Are you Austrian, or maybe German?" he said.

"French, Belgian, Jewish, Jamaican . . ." I said.

Placing two fingers on my waist, he signaled the coffee bar over the road.

Demurely, I smiled.

No sooner had we sat down than I made the excuse of needing the bathroom. Picking up my parcel, I said, "I might try it on."

"Good idea," he said, X-ray eyes flickering.

In the kitchen area at the back, I told a waitress I was being harassed. Could she let me leave by the staff exit? Out on the street, I ran to the Underground. I just made it through the doors of a waiting train, the tissue paper of the parcel damp in my hands.

Back home, I felt bad. Not about the man, or my deception, but about the crudeness of the exchange. Though a minor thing, it ripped the performance that only hours before I'd affected with brio. I felt sullied by what I'd done. It made me wonder about Sabine, if she'd have acted like that. For the first time, when I brought her to mind nothing lit up.

I hid the negligee in my cupboard. But I didn't want it in my room; I didn't want it in the flat. After a few hours, I threw it away in a public bin. I dismissed the incident, and the odd shadow it briefly cast, as an unimportant blip.

Now, it reminds me of when, as a child, I saw a strikingly pretty shell on a rock at the beach. I tried to pick it up, to add it to the collection in my bucket, but it was stuck. I knew I wasn't meant to take shells stuck to rocks, but using my spade I smashed it loose. A week later there was a terrible stink in my room. It came from the shell, the rotten creature inside. My neighbor scooped it out and washed the shell— but when he gave it back to me, I couldn't keep it. I threw it into the dam near where we lived and it sank out of sight.

30

After the negligee incident, I sought clarity. What was I doing? Why was I doing it? And what exactly did I want from Sabine? Despite his disapproval of my promiscuity, I ended up talking to Earl again. He'd asked my opinion on some tracks he was mixing.

His bedroom was like an intricate 3D puzzle perfectly constructed. Though filled with records, turntables, and computer equipment, it didn't feel crammed. Each object had its place and he kept it immaculate. There was a mild citrus scent from his shower gel. If it hadn't been for the majestic dog bed you'd never have guessed Coño slept there too.

Yet while Earl's room was a safe, ordered space, the sounds he filled it with were unrestrainedly creative. From his computer, he'd play me different versions of the same tune. Sitting on a three-legged stool across the room, I'd tell him which I preferred. He said he rated my musicality; it felt like a fun, random thing. Since there were no expectations, it was easy to go on instinct. That day, I shifted topics in the same spirit.

"Did you always know you were bisexual?" I asked.

"No," he said. "Some gay men try to be straight, then realize they aren't. With me, it was the opposite. Once I came out, I found I liked women too."

"How come?"

"A friend's sister asked me to be her date as a favor. And then we fell in love."

"So it was about one specific woman?"

"As opposed to . . . ?"

"What if you're actually gay? And she was the exception?"

He toyed with one of his twists; they were dyed purple this week. "Why choose an illogical explanation over bisexual?"

"If it's honest?"

"But you're bi, Meggie?"

"Not sure."

He slotted a new disc into the hard drive. "All those one-nighters with men put you off?"

"No, it's women I'm not sure about."

"But you and SJ are crazy for each other!"

"You reckon she's crazy for me?"

"Definitely."

I wanted to scamper off to my room. It had been like that since I was a child. Whenever someone said something nice I wanted to get away so as to preserve it.

"You're into Sabine too, though?" Earl asked.

I pressed my palms against the stool. "That's what I've been trying to work out. Am I gay, or straight, or bi? But maybe I've been asking the wrong question."

"What's the right one?"

"Is it possible in life to want to fuck just one person of the same sex?"

He frowned as the disc ejected itself; he wiped it. "Unlikely."

I said nothing.

"*Are* you into Sabine?" he asked.

"I love to watch her." I chose my words carefully. "And I want to touch her." He put the disc back in the slot. "To touch her while watching her. And I think about her constantly—"

The disc began to play but he paused it. "You want my advice?"

I nodded.

"You like men. You're into Sabine now. So you're bi."

"Mm."

"Or else a psychosexual obsessive."

"*What?*"

"Someone who's so fixated on a person or thing that their sexuality focuses on it too."

I stared at him.

He stared back, exaggeratedly. "Meggie, for fuck's sake!"

"But what if I am that?"

"You're way too sensitive. Now help me out here. Apply your sensitivity to listening for the reverb on these tracks."

He played three versions of an electronic piece recorded in a studio, a bathroom, and under a bridge.

Listening, I felt like Eve after eating the apple. My fixation with Sabine extended into every area of my life. Was that what my sexual interest in her was about? Earl was just too sunny a person to truly believe what he'd uncovered.

Then again, I wasn't driven by desire for her. More, by insatiable curiosity about her. And some impossible fantasy of being her. *It* didn't make sense—but *she* made me feel alive.

As the third track finished, Earl waited for my response.

Instinctively, I liked the version with the imperfections, the one under the bridge. But I felt wary of my openness. "The studio's best," I said.

"Really, Meggie?"

I shrugged a shoulder. "It's polished."

Earl looked disappointed. "I was *sure* you'd say the bridge. But I guess I was wrong."

31

Sabine and I made our single trip away together the week after the summer solstice. It happened swiftly, unexpectedly. In the morning, we were looking in the window of a travel agent at Victoria station; by midday, we were checking into a Georgian hotel in Eastbourne. The manager upgraded us to a top-floor suite with a clawfoot bathtub in the bedroom and a bay window filled with sea and sky.

Attracted to the shimmering town by its sweepingly grand facades, we hadn't realized we'd be a quarter of the average age. Then that became part of the adventure too. After a blustery walk along the promenade, Sabine ran us a deep bubble bath. Stripping off our clothes, we kept on the long strings of plastic granny beads we'd got in a local store.

As we climbed into the tub, steaming water rose towards the brim.

"Let's make a pact," Sabine said. "To come back here when we're eighty."

I felt pastel-mooded, lighthearted. "OK."

I didn't think she meant it. She had this way of being sincere and careless, both. "How will we seal the pact?"

"Tattoos," she said. "Seahorses."

"Where would you like yours?"

Languidly, she arched her slender foot against the rim of the bath. I traced a seahorse figure on the side of her sole. "Here?" I said. Rivulets of water trickled from her muscled calf into the tuck of her knee. "Or here . . . ?" I followed them down the back of her thigh.

At the bubbles that hid the rest of her, I stopped. The skin of her shoulders, her neck, her cheeks was radiant and dewy. Her eyes were half closed but she was watching me through her lashes.

I tossed my hair, feeling damp burnished spirals framing my face. Our beads floated on the water: mine green, hers white. Two flappers from the nineteen twenties. Chorus girls on a clandestine break.

I turned the taps off behind me. If she wanted something to happen between us, it was her turn to make a move.

Water ran into the overflow pipe.

Then she said, "You hardly ever talk about your mother."

"No."

"You don't get on?"

"We're different," I said. "We think differently."

"What's she like?"

Narcissistic was the word that came to mind. But I wanted to keep things light. I told her how my surname, Groenewald, was common in South Africa but my mother didn't pronounce it the usual way. Depending on her audience, sometimes she anglicized it, claiming she was Mrs. Greenfields; other times, with foreigners, she preceded it with "von" for an aristocratic spin.

"Meggie Greenfields?"

"Meggie von Groenewald to you, Sabine."

"What does your mother do for a living?" she asked.

"Florist," I said. "Or rather, she owns a flower shop."

"What's the difference?"

"Thandi, who works for her, does the arranging. She makes beautiful understated bouquets. My mother gives them *flair*. So if Thandi ties up a bunch of baby's breath and pink rosebuds, my mother will add a *striking strelitzia*. Or if Thandi fills a basket with Namaqualand daisies, my mother will poke in a *swizzy grasshopper* on a stick."

"She sounds like a character."

"You could put it that way."

Thandi was the reason the shop survived. And yet my mother treated her as its weakest link. If the flowers weren't properly stored or the orders were incorrect, Thandi got the blame. As a teenager, the only times I'd crossed my mother were to defend Thandi but whenever I did, she'd get annoyed and defend my mother in turn. My mother's superpower was to make allies of those who by right should have been her enemies.

Sabine slanted her eyes at me. "It's hard not to have a father."

Ordinarily, I'd correct people, saying it wasn't hard, or sad, or whatever they'd assumed because I'd never known him. But the way Sabine said it made me ask, hesitantly, "Is your father . . . ?"

"Does your mother have other servants?" she said.

"Thandi isn't her servant," I said. "But she has a cleaner twice a week." I left out that she also had a weekly gardener.

"My mother is a cleaner," said Sabine.

"Of houses?"

"Offices. My father was a bricklayer."

Was?

"He left when I was eight."

"*That's* tough," I said.

"My mother made his life hell. But she knows how to make the other person believe they are the bad one. She can make someone feel so shit they want to die."

My mother could do that too, though I'd never told anybody.

"Living in a different country to your family has advantages," I said.

"Does your mother beg you to visit?" Sabine asked.

"No," I said. "Does yours?"

"She says I owe her. But I hate to do it. She calls me a Jezebel, blames me for everything. When I'm not with her, I feel sorry for her. But when I'm there . . ."

"I know what you mean," I said. "My mother and I are not estranged, but almost. On the phone I feel guilty. But when I'm with her, I feel trapped. I don't think she likes the real me very much."

"Do you like the real her?"

I took a shaky breath, shrugged. Even with it being six years since I'd first left home for university, I still felt my mother's monitoring presence.

The hot tap was dripping; I tried to screw it tighter. It was like we were in a bad mother competition. When I turned back to Sabine, I flicked some bubbles at her.

"Sometimes I can see you as a child," she said.

"What sort of child?"

"Fiercely loyal, a dreamer. Eager to please." Her eyes shone; she looked like she was about to say more, then shook her head.

"What sort of child were you?" I asked.

"Guess."

What came to mind was *sexy*. But I couldn't say that. "Not eager to please."

She looked hurt. "I *was* eager to please my brother."

She bit one of her tiny fingernails. Then she said, "My mother chased him away too. Said he was a bad influence."

"Was he?"

She didn't answer at once. Then she held up two fingers,

crossed. "We were like this. Xavier loved me more than life itself. He told me, 'I love you more than life itself.'"

"How old was he when he left?"

"Seventeen. I was twelve."

"Does Xavier look like you?"

"He looked . . . like Jacques Brel."

I reached for her hand and held it.

"After my mother kicked him out, Xavier didn't care about living. He started to free-climb, high up, without ropes."

"I've seen it on TV," I said.

"Then he did BASE jumping. I thought he'd die BASE jumping. But he didn't."

I gripped her hand tightly.

"He dived off a high rock into a pool," she said. "His friends did it, everybody did it. It was a place known for this. You won't die unless you fall sideways and hit the rock. Or aim for the rock. People say, it's safe, you'd have to be aiming for the rock."

Bath water splashed over the sides as I put my arms around Sabine. I stroked her silky black hair. I held her, and she held me. Our bellies touched, our breasts, our cheeks. I wanted to kiss her then, but recalled times with men when they'd converted an emotional moment into an opportunity for sex. How even when it was tender, I'd had this sense of rewarding their empathy, that they'd been hoping for the reward. It made me feel detached, slightly more alone. Not a big thing—forgivable even. But I didn't want Sabine to feel like that. I didn't want her to feel alone at all.

When Sabine let go of me, the way she did it was solicitous. As if she was the comforter, the one comforting me. She smoothed my forehead and kissed my cheek: a dry, maternal kiss.

Then she heaved herself out of the tub with both arms. "Water's cold."

I stared at the hole in the bubbles as she traipsed across the carpet, confused.

After she closed the bathroom door, I sat on the bed wrapped in a thick, white towel. From the bathroom came the roar of the hairdryer. I went to the door and pressed my ear to it, sure I'd hear Sabine's crying behind the dryer's noise. But I heard only the dryer, then silence, then the dryer again.

With dinner in the hotel's smart restaurant included in our deal, we'd packed clothes to match. Waiting for Sabine, I put on the sea-green dress I'd worn to the ballet with my silver slingback heels.

When she finally emerged, she was in a diaphanous lilac gown that trailed to her ankles. I didn't understand why she'd needed to dress privately. As she sat at the mirror, trying to fasten her scarab pendant, her fingers were trembling.

"Hungry?" I asked, going over to her.

She shook her head.

After I'd fastened the clasp, she said she felt ill. When I asked what was wrong, her expression was disconsolate. With my hands on her shoulders, I told her we didn't have to go down to eat. We could do whatever she wanted to do.

Her muscles relaxed, her relief palpable. She said she wanted to take a sleeping pill and go to bed.

Since I didn't fancy lying awake beside her, or eating downstairs on my own, I took the pill she offered me too. Side by side, we stretched out on the ivory covers of the enormous divan in our long dinner dresses. I went from staring at the stucco patterns on the ceiling to feeling the sharp glare of sunlight pressing at my eyelids.

The phone was ringing; it was reception. The pills, stronger than any I'd had before, must have hit instantly. We'd overslept and it was already two P.M. The staff needed us to check out so that they could clean the room.

Afterwards, I wasn't sure how to think of the trip. Certainly I knew more about Sabine and she about me. But I was also unsettled by it. At the age of five, I'd had a friend who got too homesick to cope with sleepovers. Normally a confident child, she would tremble and sob until she threw up. Sabine's need for the sleeping pills reminded me of that.

32

Back in London, Eastbourne got stored in the miscellaneous section of my memory. The chest for arbitrarily recalled dreams, unjustified predictions. Meanwhile things between Sabine and me returned to normal. Better than normal: closer, warmer. As the last summer of the century progressed, our uneven journey continued—but now with a soundtrack to match.

We both had similarly eclectic taste; I was always either listening to an album she'd burned for me or finding one to burn for her. But recently she'd started a little game by slipping PJ Harvey's "Is This Desire?" in among the tracks of a Tricky album. It was typical Sabine: surprises, contradictions. One moment I was listening to a complex low-tempo groove, the next to a lone female voice with guitar and drum.

In response, I slotted "Kiss Me" by Sixpence None the Richer in among Bach's cello suites. She put "Kiss You All Over" by Exile into an album by Kate Bush. I put James Brown's "Please, Please, Please" onto a Debussy album. She put "I'm Your Man" by Leonard Cohen into Missy Elliott's *Supa Dupa Fly* . . .

Applying myself fully to our project, I used music shops as lending libraries when my money ran out. I assumed Sabine did the same, though she never said. Money wasn't a topic that came up, nor did I want it to; financial complaints sat cheek by jowl with materialistic aspirations in my mother's world. Her chief bugbear was that my father had died before insuring his life. *We could have been like Mrs. Esterhuizen, with her new BMW every year and her overseas trips. And her husband wasn't even a lecturer.*

Alternating extravagance with extreme frugality, I got by—until one day, I didn't. I was a hundred pounds short on my August rent. It wasn't a huge amount but I had no way of raising it. That night at work, *money money money* was all that was on my mind. I hoped to get through the shift without having to talk to anyone. But in the early hours, I got stuck in a lift with Sherry, Lizard, the shift leader, and Sabine. Huddling to myself, I shut my eyes.

"Love your outfit, SJ," the shift leader said.

Today it was a black net top under a grungy slip dress.

"Everything looks good on you," Sherry added. "D'you ever do modeling?"

I opened one eye; Sabine was shaking her head.

"You and her, both," Sherry said, referring to the shift leader, "could be models. Whereas me and Meggie are girl-next-door types."

I opened my other girl-next-door eye. What Sherry had said was true. The shift leader's hair was loose; crimped, it rippled onto her shoulders. She had a smudge of maroon shadow on her eyelids. Sabine wore no makeup but her lips were as red as if tinted, her lashes as black as if kohled.

"Girl-next-door types are the best," said Lizard.

"Yeah, and my favorite bird's a pigeon," I said.

"Is it?" said Sherry.

"No," I said.

Sabine laughed. "Pigeons are pretty, pearly at the neck."

"I prefer blue tits," said Lizard.

"Did I hear tits?" Prawn shouted from outside of the lift.

"You are so missing out, Prawny," Sherry said.

Wedging a large screwdriver between the lift doors, Prawn prised them open a centimeter. His white-fringed eye appeared in the gap. Lizard joked that it was like we were in a peep show. Prawn latched on to the idea as *da bomb*.

While the others laughed it off, I cleared my throat.

"What d'you want to peep at?" I asked Prawn.

"You and Sabine. Kissing."

"OK," I said.

"OK?" Sabine raised her eyebrows.

"For money," I said.

"You didn't charge before," Prawn said.

"Wasn't a peep show before," I said.

Sabine was studying me.

"How much?" said Prawn.

"Twenty to start," I said. "Rolled tight, and slotted through the gap."

"*Twenty quid?* I haven't got twenty pee!"

"No twenty, no peep," I said.

"Aw . . ." said Prawn.

"I've got an idea," Sabine said. "We'll do the kissy peep show for you, if you do one for us first."

"No, I veto that," I said.

Why . . . ? mouthed Sabine.

"Hang on," said the shift leader. "This is getting interesting."

"Beg, borrow, or steal, but cough up," I said firmly.

"*I'll* do it with Sabine," the shift leader said to Prawn, "if you do it for us first."

Inside a tune twisted; since the hypnosis night some months back, I'd suspected she wanted this.

"Do—what?" said Prawn.

"Kiss a bloke," said the shift leader.

"I've never done that."

"First time for everything," said Sherry.

"But who can I ask?" said Prawn, his eye blinking. "Lizard?"

"I'm in here, mate. Can't do it through the peep."

In the silence, we heard footsteps in the corridor.

Prawn's eye left the hole, then came back. "Göker?"

Göker was a hairy, butch guy from Energy. Though he never came out drinking with us, from the marinade of his eyes and skin I'd assumed he took alcoholism to a level that made us seem like children.

"Don't even go there," I warned Prawn.

But the shift leader seemed to have lost her head at the prospect of kissing Sabine.

"Ask Göker, Prawn," she instructed.

We heard Prawn walk off.

Sherry's lips stretched with anxiety.

Next thing, big, butch Göker came over. His bullish eye roamed across us. He tried to pry open the lift doors.

I smiled; Prawn had bottled it, Göker had come to rescue us.

The gap between the doors widened a few more centimeters before the screwdriver snapped. Göker tossed the two pieces aside.

"Now you can all see," he said, beaming.

Göker and Prawn faced each other. Göker stood as upright

as a guard. Prawn moved in, pulling a constipated face. At first, it was like bad porn; then Göker put his hands on either side of Prawn's pale head and kissed him, hard. Prawn seemed momentarily almost swept away. Göker broke the kiss off with a laugh.

"Good enough?" he asked us.

"Thanks, mate," said Prawn, moving his hand to wipe his mouth, then thinking better of it.

Göker thumped his shoulder, and left.

"Is he gay?" said the shift leader.

"Maybe gay, maybe bi," said Lizard.

"Whatever," said Sabine. "He's cool."

"So's Prawny," said Sherry. "The nineties aren't exactly the swinging sixties!"

Sabine winked at me; grudgingly, I winked back.

Prawn filled the gap between the lift doors with his shiny pink face. "Swinging or not, I'm getting a fucking *deckchair*. You girls owe me big time."

"*Pas de problème*," said the shift leader. She turned to Sabine. "Is that the right expression?"

"*Oui*," said Sabine.

Pas de problème. Oui.

The shift leader draped one slim arm around Sabine, then the other. Sabine glanced at me. She mouthed, *Shall I say no?*

I shook my head, surprised. She kept looking at me while the shift leader did flitty kisses up her neck. I didn't know what face to make; I wanted to watch, I didn't want to watch. *Close your eyes*, I mouthed to her.

Prawn's chair squeaked as he opened it out.

"Start again!" he shouted. "I'm back!"

Sabine closed her eyes and they kissed. A long, sensuous, aesthetically pleasing kiss. I pretended they were models on a photo shoot.

But I didn't need to pretend. When they broke apart, I didn't feel jealous. Sabine's eyes were on me, her lips asking, *You OK?*

I knew then I was her girl at work if I wanted it.

Yet when I tried to smile back, to reassure her, *Yes, of course*, I was overwhelmed by a sense I didn't deserve her. I wasn't beautiful like a model. I didn't do my job well, wasn't able to get a degree, couldn't even be counted on to have the money for rent. Not to mention maybe being a psychosexual obsessive . . .

Feeling like an altogether inferior species, I sought the solitude of the lavatories the moment we were released from the lift. Locked into the far cubicle, I cried. Then I kicked the wall. I shoved a toilet roll into my mouth and screamed.

Sabine's white face appeared at the top of the cubicle divider.

Over a mug of horrible French herb tea on a back staircase, I gave the most straightforward explanation for my behavior. I told Sabine I'd been overspending. Things had spiraled out of control. The bank sent a letter. I didn't open it for two days. Then I did. The more I spoke, the more my words hit home. I had penalty charges for overdrawing. My credit card was maxed. But that wasn't the worst of it.

"What's the worst?" she asked.

"Tomorrow's rent day. I'm a hundred quid short."

"Earl will understand, Meggie."

"It's not up to *Earl*. He doesn't own the flat."

"Is this really just about money?"

"Yes!"

"You weren't making a hundred-pound noise in there. You were bankrupted."

I frowned at her.

She touched my arm. "Don't worry, it's not the end of the world."

"Just the end of my rent. Next week I'll be on the streets."

She shook her head. "Something will work out."

The rest of that night, I didn't listen to music. Wherever I went, Sabine was chatting away. Relieved she didn't attempt to include me in her gaiety, I kept my head down.

At last, the interminable shift came to an end. But as I was leaving the warehouse, she ran up to me. She pressed a paper bag into my hand.

I unfolded the top; it was filled with notes.

"We had a little whip round—"

"Sabine, I can't accept this!"

"Pay the rent"—she turned back to the building—"then buy us a drink."

After work the next morning, I went to the White Hart. Sabine wasn't there. I tried to buy everyone else a drink, but they wouldn't hear of it. While there'd been over a hundred pounds in the bag, they insisted they'd contributed no more than a couple of pounds each. Maybe they had.

And maybe they hadn't.

33

After Sabine's kiss with the shift leader, I wondered if anything would develop between them. She'd been reassuring in the lift, though that was before she saw me in the loos. But, miraculously, neither drama nor irresponsibility appeared to have put her off. On the contrary, she embedded *two* rogue tracks into a metalcore album: "Déshabillez-moi" by Juliette Gréco and "I'll Make Love to You" by Boyz II Men. I'd chosen Schubert's "Liebesbotschaft" as my first reply; the other I planned to select following the solar eclipse.

Sabine and I had made arrangements to watch it together. We had the protective sunglasses provided free with the daily papers, and a bucket of water to reflect the phenomenon too. Earl had gone off to Cornwall so we had his balcony to ourselves. I'd read that the earth would go dark, cold, and quiet. Birds would return to their nests; bats would flit across the sky.

Despite the New Cross sky being solidly overcast, as Sabine and I held hands, I felt the buildup of something momentous. The muggy August air began to cool, the mid-morning light to dim . . . We looked from the clouds to the water in the bucket, to the clouds again. Through the orange tint of the cardboard glasses, Sabine resembled a nerdy person caught on old film negatives. Seeing her like that gave me courage for my secret plan: to kiss her at the moment the earth went dark.

With the handicap of being sober, I should've gone through my moves. Would I slide a hand around her waist, then draw her to me and kiss her neck? Or would I take her cheeks in my palms and brush her lips with mine? Instead, I thought of how she always seemed like someone slightly different; I could never get to the bottom of her. She was perceptive, intuitive, and compassionate. The sort of person who did things without fussing. I admired her streetwise savvy and how she was also kind.

So my paean to Sabine continued until the sky began to get lighter. I hauled the glasses off and stared brazenly into the sun. "Was that *it*?"

"*Oui, mon chouchou.*"

I couldn't believe it. In place of the thick cover of darkness I'd been counting on, the experience felt like no more than driving in and out of the shadow of a mountain.

Unceremoniously, I tried to take Sabine's glasses off too.

"Wait," she said, stopping me. "I'm still looking."

"Nothing's there. Look at me, rather."

Amused, she held the boxy glasses back from her face.

I leaned in, intending one of our deep, intimate kisses. But then I saw she wasn't expecting it. Her lips were closed. I was too late to make my lips do a peck. So I sort of breathed on her with my open mouth, then ran away, embarrassed, into the flat.

She came running after me, giggling. "Poor Meggie!"

"Poor Sabine!"

"But you had Great Expectations, no?"

In my room, we both collapsed onto my mattress. My side was by the street; hers by the door. She opened a bag of chewy sweets and threw me one. I threw it back. Her eyes teased; I felt silly. Everything seemed like a tease that I took too seriously: our kisses, the tracks we swapped, "Déshabillez-moi."

While she busied herself with her phone, I reached behind the blackout curtain to open the window. As the cloth flapped against the glass the room was never dark, just more shadowy or less.

A truck below blasted out rap lyrics to the tune of "Jesus Loves Me." *Wha's yo mutherfukkin game? Wha's yo mutherfukkin game? Don mess wit me . . .*

When she put her phone away, I asked, "Where's Louche today? Lucian?"

"Fuck knows."

"Is that what you call him for short?"

"No."

"D'you call him *mon chouchou*?"

She tossed her head. "I call him Papa."

"He likes that?"

157

"*I* do."

The truck hadn't moved; it was caught in a traffic jam. *Wha's yo mutherfukkin game? Don mess wit me, yo JHC . . .*

"What does he call you?" I asked.

"My girl."

My girl was different to *My Sabine*. It could be innocent, like the soul song. Or it could be dark. I stared hard at Sabine in the dimness. Then I looked down at the childish feet sticking out of my jeans; at moments my own body could seem equally foreign. *Who is she, this woman in my bed?*

"Tell me a fact from your teenage years," I said.

"You go first," she said.

"I was a Christian," I said. "It was everything to me."

"And then—it just stopped?"

"At university, I met people from other religions. When I saw how strongly they believed in their gods, Christianity didn't make sense anymore. It's the same with relationships, I guess. If I realize it's not happening, I shut the door."

The truck had moved on. Sitar music was coming from a colorful campervan. I expected Sabine might offer up something spiritual.

But she said, "One summer I had to go to hospital by the sea."

I thought of her dancing. "For your feet?"

"Don't like to say."

"In Belgium?"

"No. *En Suède.* Sweden, the islands."

The campervan was stuck in the traffic jam now.

158

"They made us do tiring things," she continued. "Though we also swam in the lakes. Sat around a big fire. Talked, told stories. Sometimes what we said was true, sometimes not. But lies can be . . . more true than the truth."

I held the blackout cloth back.

"What are you thinking now?" I asked.

"I like the music."

"Me too. I wonder what it is?"

"But, Meggie. What matters isn't the facts. It's how our lives cross when we're together. This changes us, makes us unstable—"

"Unstable?"

"It's good," she said. "Exciting."

The sitar music moved on; the conversation felt harder to continue without the soundtrack. I wished the campervan would come back.

"Impermanence is life," I said, letting the blackout cloth drop.

"Sleep is life too." Sabine yawned.

A few minutes later, I could hear the soft rhythm of her breath. In the shifting grays of the room, I watched her: the line of her back, her neck, her hair. The wonder of another person. I felt something retract. It was pointless to try to push the physical boundary between us. I promised myself not to initiate anything again. What I had was enough.

34

Around this time, Sabine appeared to have moved. Where she'd lived previously was grim: a run-down terrace in Peckham with a flaking green door. I'd glimpsed an empty hallway and a stack of unopened post. She'd said the house belonged to an elderly woman and her rented room was shabby, that I'd be shocked by how shabby it was. She didn't say much else about her landlady other than that having friends over would be an invasion of her space. Not interested in invading anyone's space, I'd text Sabine when I got there and wait for her in the street.

I never saw another person enter or leave the building. Though I do recall a gray, blustery day and the metallic, sickly smell of the butcher's shop opposite. How it troubled me to watch men unloading the milky-white carcasses from behind the plastic fronds of their frosty van.

Shortly after the eclipse, Sabine began texting me to swing by a smart Georgian mansion block in Mayfair instead. A black wrought-iron fence framed a couple of steps that led up to a studded double door. Antique lanterns were mounted on either side of it. In the arch between them hung the building number: 29. To the left was a brass intercom system that I never used. As with the place in Peckham, I'd send a message when I arrived and she'd come down.

Apparently the place was Lucian's. Sabine pointed to a window at the right corner; his studio flat was up there on the second floor. He required a bolt-hole away from the family home to work on his latest novel. As soon as she left he had to get on; he hardly needed the distraction of her bringing me upstairs with her. "He likes you, though," she said. "He thinks you're lovely."

I grimaced at the word. "Are you and he getting more serious, then?"

"Not really."

"You're always there nowadays."

"We used to go to hotels. Now it's not necessary."

"I didn't pick you up from hotels."

"Obviously not, Meggie."

Then she said that the mansion block was an odd place. She hadn't met any of their neighbors. The whole building seemed to be owned by rich people from other countries who were never around. "Most of the time it's dead quiet inside," she said.

"Suits Papa," she added.

After I ran out of money, I'd give Earl my rent in advance, the day I got paid. The rest of the month I'd leave to balance itself, prioritizing times with Sabine. For each adventure we had, whoever made the suggestion funded it. Mostly we alternated, though sometimes I'd do a few in a row or vice versa. Since I didn't feel used and wasn't using Sabine, I assumed it worked out reciprocally.

Occasionally, before she went back to the Mayfair flat,

Sabine suggested ending the night at Claridge's. We'd be warmly greeted by staff as we went in. She'd waltz up to the bar and ask for two glasses of Cristal. Because of its silly spelling, I assumed it was cheap. She'd insist it was her treat and I'd let her enjoy being generous. We'd take our favorite table; then she'd repeat the order and we'd Cristal the night away.

Once, I suggested ending an evening with a date similarly. I finished my glass of Cristal in no time, though he seemed to be taking inordinately long with his. When the waiter came round and I asked for another, my date said, "How about a cocktail this time?"

"OK," I said.

"Two mojitos," he said.

When the waiter had disappeared, I said, "Don't you like Cristal?"

He looked a bit sheepish. "I'm thinking of the bill."

"I'll get it—"

"No, no."

"Of course I will," I said. "But why d'you order cocktails if you're worried?"

"They're cheaper than Cristal."

"No way," I said.

"Bet you the next round of cocktails!"

"You mean the next round of Cristal!"

He opened the drinks menu. On the third page, he showed me—cocktails, mojito: twelve pounds. I smiled while he carried on flipping the pages. When he reached the last page, he turned the menu around. He pointed at Cristal: fifty pounds. That was way more than I'd expected. But at fifty a bottle, a glass would still probably be cheaper than a cocktail.

"No," he said, "it's per glass."

I checked; he was right.

Astonished, I paged through the menu again, trying to find a different way to interpret it. When the waiter returned with our mojitos, to my date's embarrassment I asked, "Is this the price?"

"Yes," the waiter said.

"Has it always cost that much?"

"It's Cristal," he said. "And, darling, you *are* in Claridge's."

After he'd gone, I said, "My friend buys us rounds and rounds of the stuff every time we're here."

"Your friend must really want to impress you," he said.

35

Cal Janssen was someone I'd had a crush on for half my life. He was tanned, rangy, and blond with lake-blue eyes. At school I'd gone out with his softer-featured younger brother. We'd both worshipped Cal and he'd been consistently kind to us.

On holiday in Gordon's Bay when I was twenty, I'd bumped into Cal at a beach party. Skinny-dipping in the sea, he'd said he fancied me. I'd said I fancied him too. Our sex was briefly intoxicating. But he called the next day to

Kiare Ladner

say what we'd done was, *Not cool, Meggie.* Although I didn't think it was that terrible, I pretended to agree.

I'd assumed that'd be the last I'd see of Cal, but we seemed destined to bump into each other randomly. On a hot September night when Sabine and I were in a Chinatown dive bar it happened again. He left his group of blokeish guys to drink with us. When they moved on elsewhere, he stayed. He said they were colleagues from the architects' firm where he worked. He was involved in a project on social housing: eco, sustainable stuff. He asked what we did for a living. Sabine excelled herself in making our jobs sound important and us indispensable. We drank more shots together, made silly toasts, laughed, told stories, and smoked.

Shortly before the bar closed, Sabine followed me to the bathroom. Adding a coat of mascara, she said, "He's hot."

"You fancy him?"

"You do too."

"No way."

"I know you do!" Turning from her reflection, she put her arms around me. "Let's have a threesome."

Despite the undercurrent at the Opera House, Sabine hadn't suggested anything like this before. *She must like him a lot*, I thought.

Back in our candlelit corner, I weighed it up. On the one hand, it'd be fun. On the other, I didn't want Sabine to have sex with me just because she wanted it with him. I didn't want pity sex from her; if it happened between us, it needed to be completion sex. But there was also an invisible third

164

hand to the problem: I didn't want Cal to say again, and in front of Sabine, *Not cool, Meggie.*

I considered telling Sabine about Gordon's Bay. I trusted that she'd prioritize our friendship. That she'd change the direction of the evening to one of tease-not-touch revenge.

Yet, as I waited at the bar watching the pair of them take such obvious pleasure in each other, I thought maybe Papa wasn't good for Sabine. Maybe she needed someone like Cal. Maybe with him she'd be happier than she could ever imagine. After all, who wouldn't be?

When Cal went outside to take a call, I told Sabine I was tired, exhausted; I had a cold coming on. I didn't fancy him but, definitely, she should—

"Meggie, you're lying."

"No. He's a great guy—"

"But?"

I sighed. "I'm not doing it, Sabine. But you want to. And I want you to."

When Cal came back downstairs I slipped off the bench. Planting kisses on each of their cheeks, I left.

The night bus home was noisy with drunken teenagers and stinky with stale farts. When I tried to look out the window, the reflection of the interior blocked the city beyond. At my feet the floor was sticky; an orange can rolled to and fro.

I'd given Sabine a long-term boyfriend, a fiancé, a husband. Already I could see her simple white dress, her slender hands holding frangipanis. She and Cal would be as infatuated with each other as I'd been with each of them. They'd have kids together, rangy and beautiful, a boy and a girl. Emigrating to Canada, they'd live by a lake in a wooden eco house, designed and built by themselves. I'd visit, bearing gifts for the little Janssens. Meggie, the London godmother. No more than the character in their fairy tale who'd brought them together.

When I didn't hear from Sabine the next morning, I went for a run to Crystal Palace. Then I took a bracingly cold shower. Afterwards I played Bill Evans's *Conversations with Myself*, which I hadn't listened to in a long while.

I imagined a room with a black futon bed beneath a window shaded by a bamboo blind. Sabine wouldn't be curled into herself like she was with me. Her and Cal's bodies would be shadow-striped in the early light, their limbs tangled together.

I switched Bill off, then tidied my room. I tried to read a few pages of the Jean Rhys novel I'd had in my rucksack for months. Nothing from Sabine.

Twelve o'clock, one o'clock, two o'clock, nothing. I left the flat and walked two hours to Hyde Park. In the café by the Serpentine, I allowed myself to be chatted up by a greasy, lank-haired man. I let him have my number with no digits altered. Five minutes later, I got a text. *PrT, Brighton, 2nite.*

166

Driving down. Wn2 come? I walked home, checking my phone. Every ten minutes, every five. But it was always only more texts from the Serpentine man. *U SxC gal. PrT b orsum! I cn pik u up? Gud tyms :) :)*

Back at my flat, I finally texted Sabine. *how're things*

ok, she texted back. Then, *i could come round now ish*

lets go out rather. I wanted the armor of public surroundings. *pig and hen at 9*

ok

I dressed in black jeans and a lace cami. I blow-dried my hair to make it sleek and took time over my makeup. When I saw her, I was glad of the effort I'd made because it seemed she'd done the same. She was all in black too, eyelashes curled, lips glossed.

I set a glass of red wine in front of her with my hands trembling a little, like hers sometimes did. I was so sure of what I was about to hear.

So sure that I made her repeat what she'd said twice.

She claimed it had been fine, all right. Cal wasn't really her type either. "Like you said, Meggie, he's a nice enough guy."

36

The Pig and Hen was out of cigarettes so I nipped to a mini supermarket a couple of doors down. As I joined the queue by the cigs and booze counter, I looked, and looked again.

Graham, my ex-boyfriend, was standing there in fruit and veg, dressed in a charcoal suit. I'd not seen him in a suit before but he filled it out; he looked amazingly good in it.

Since, thanks to my earlier efforts, I felt okayish too, I dared myself to go up to him. Maybe he'd say get lost—but probably he wouldn't. Our disastrous end had been such a small part of the relationship as a whole. Besides, even if Sabine's night with Cal hadn't worked out, some day she'd meet a single guy with whom it would. I wanted that for her, and I wanted it for myself too. Then again, quite possibly I'd *already* met my guy. In hindsight, what I'd had with Graham was pretty rare. We'd been intimate, able to talk about anything, even shared a sense of humor.

I'd just left my place in the queue when Graham tossed a bunch of flowers into his basket. A large unambiguous bouquet of oxblood roses. For a moment, I stood stuck between cigs and booze, and fruit and veg. Then, he saw me. Unquestionably, he saw me. But his eyes kept moving. They moved on as evenly as if I were no more significant than the 2-for-1 toilet roll promotion by the cleaning materials aisle, which was where he headed next.

Cheeks flaming, I abandoned the cigarettes along with my temporary delusion. I tried to walk in as nonchalant a manner as possible back to the pub.

A few drinks later, seeking distraction from the fading supermarket scene, I asked Sabine if she fancied partying with the

Serpentine guy. Showing her his messages, I told her he was safely neither of our types. I expected the texts to put her off but to my surprise she was up for it. So I sent him a reply: *I'd like 2 brng sum1. Cn U pik us both up?*

Immediately my phone beeped. *SxC gal like u?*

I groaned. "He's a creep. Let's leave it."

Sabine flipped the phone around.

With a half-smile, she texted him back: *SxCR*

Forty minutes later a two-tone army-green car with a turbo exhaust roared past us. At the bottom of the road, it reversed and came back. It screeched to a halt where we stood outside the Pig and Hen. The stereo was thudding with drum and bass; when the Serpentine guy opened the doors, the night pounded with it. I felt a wave of affection for his exuberance. He'd spruced up by ponytailing his hair and dousing himself in acrylic cologne. *"Laydeez!"*

We squeezed in together on the front seat. The dashboard was flecked with what could have been dandruff but a couple of blocks on was confirmed as coke. He pulled into a deserted alley under a graffitied archway behind a building site. By the white light of a security lamp, we snorted lines as thick as pupae. The pungency of Serp Guy's cologne in the stationary car almost made us sneeze them right out. Holding our noses closed, we waved to the security cameras.

As we hit the outskirts of the city, the streets became wider and darker and quieter. The night sky was shifting black; the moon and stars were smothered by roiling cloud. At the last traffic lights before the highway, Serp Guy took three acid tabs from the glove compartment. He gave us one each. Sabine ejected his drum and bass CD and flung it into the back.

In the silence, I had a plunging moment of misgiving. Driving on coke was one thing but driving on LSD? I remembered an anti-drugs film we'd been shown in high school. With an eye on the red traffic light, I lifted the doorknob. Sabine and I could get out here, we could run; if we went in the opposite direction to the traffic he couldn't follow us.

As "The Sunshine Underground" came onto the car stereo, Sabine took my hand away from the door. She put my fingers, clutching the tab of LSD, into her mouth. The traffic light turned orange; it flashed and I released the tab. She kissed my fingers, then put her tab into my mouth. The light went green. I thought, *I have chosen.* I thought, *I have seen the future and I have chosen this.* And then, as if I were following something already scripted over which I had no control, I was no longer afraid. I helped Sabine open the sunroof wide as the car accelerated off onto the open river of black tar.

While the journey continued, we played trippy electronic themes full blast. Tricky, Chemical Brothers, Kraftwerk . . . Once the tabs kicked in, we stayed mostly in the slow lane, though it didn't feel slow. The speedometer said thirty, forty, but it felt like we were flying; the world was rushing at us in party streamers of brightness. When we stopped on the hard shoulder to snort more coke, the car lights diffused into magical patterns. I could have gazed at them forever. But

Sabine and Serp Guy insisted that we move back through the portal into the traffic flow that led to the sea.

Somewhere in what really did seem like a euphoric channel of floating lights between cities, Sabine stood up on the front seat. Her legs were underwater roots while her body reached through the sunroof like a translucent white water lily. When I stood and made myself a flower too, wedged alongside her with my pincushion protea-orange hair tailing out, a scene from the anti-drugs film came back to me. Two teenagers high on acid were driving a car through the mountains. As they rounded a cliff bend, instead of slowing down, they accelerated and the car took off from the road. It flew into the air in slow motion while they held hands high above their heads, shouting, *WEEEeeeeee.*

For a reason I'd never fathomed, I'd always envied them that moment. Now, although there were no mountains let alone cliffs around, I yelled into the night at the top of my lungs, "WEEEeeeeee."

When Sabine joined me, I took her hand and held it tight above our heads.

Together, the two of us yelled as loud as we could, "WEEEeeeeee, WEEEeeeeee, WEEEeeeeee . . ."

The night didn't end as we'd expected. We drove for hours but got nowhere. Or rather, we got to Mornington Crescent. When I saw the Tube station sign, I realized we either hadn't left London or else had somehow returned. Serp Guy painstakingly negotiated the back streets of Camden but something in his driving style must have seemed off. Next thing we knew, a police car was careering towards us, sirens, lights, everything. To Serp Guy's credit, his reaction was extremely generous. He skidded around a corner, flung open the passenger door, and said, "*Laydeez, run!*"

Sabine and I didn't need any convincing; we left him to take the rap and skadoodled. Terrified of being caught, instead of running, we marched through the streets like soldiers—Sabine said soldiers were the people least likely to be arrested—until we got to Primrose Hill. It was a welcome swath of darkness, with a path lit up by what appeared to be a line of small moons.

"Shall we leave earth, Sabine?" I said. "Shall we venture into the beyond?"

"I will do it with you, Meggie." Sabine took a couple of steps towards the first moon. She looked back and reached out her hand. "Will you do it with me?"

"*Where you go I will go, and where you stay I will stay,*" I said. "*Your people will be my people and your God my God.*"

I took Sabine's hand and we began to follow the moons dot-to-dot up the hill. At moon three or four, Sabine said, "Say it again, what you just said."

I did, adding, "*Where you die I will die, and there I will be buried.*"

"That's the most beautiful thing I ever heard," she said.

"It just came to me," I said.

172

"You are a poet," said Sabine.

"No, it's the Bible."

"Oh."

We had reached the top of Primrose Hill. Below us lay the spread of its dark pelt, spotted green where the moons lit it. Beyond lay all of London.

"You must remember this," said Sabine.

"My mind's a sieve," I said.

"No, Meggie. You have a beautiful mind."

"You have a beautiful everything."

"What's an *everything*?"

I pointed mock-seriously into the distance. "The BT Tower. And Canary Wharf. And that big hoop they just put up—"

"London's Eye," she said.

"Everything's the stars," I said, "the sun, and the moon."

In the distance, a lion roared.

We stared at each other, confused.

"Everything is London Zoo," she said, triumphantly.

We started to giggle.

I knelt down on the grass; she knelt opposite me.

I lifted her tank top. "Your beautiful everything is your belly button." I lifted the top higher. "And your ribs." I pulled it over her head and flung it aside. "It's your breasts." I unhooked her bra. "And your shoulders." I tossed the bra into the dark too.

She was an ancient sculpture, a carved goddess. Totemic against the skyline, but breathing, alive. I ran my fingers wonderingly over her.

She popped the buttons of my jeans open slowly, one by one. "Yours is your hips." She kissed my panty line. "And your bum." She gave it a pinch, then slipped her fingers into my pants. "And your . . ."

I slid my hands down the front of her skirt. She wasn't wearing knickers.

"Your ruby," I said.

"Your pearl," she said.

We were solemn. She shut her eyes, I mine. While we began to feel each other's secret folds and ripples, my lives near and far, internal and external, present and past came together in a moment that felt holy.

Then we both froze.

Footsteps were clacking up the path. Too scared to look, I listened. They became muffled as they went across the grass. I tried to will them away. But they strode determinedly closer.

"Come on, girls," said a stern voice. "What's happening here? What are you two up to? This is a public place, you know?"

"Is she real?" I asked Sabine.

"Unfortunately, yes," said the policewoman.

She handed Sabine her top and her bra. Then firmly, though with a crinkle of compassion at her eyes, she gave us a talk about the wrongs of doing what we were doing in the place we were doing it.

Sabine dressed with insouciance; I tried to do the same.

But after that, the magic of the night disintegrated. Like when they switch on the lights in a club and suddenly everybody is worn out and overdressed and smells of acrid drug sweat. And your energy is so low that getting home feels like the last leg of an ill-advised expedition that you'd be better off doing alone.

As we left Primrose Hill, neither Sabine nor I spoke. It wasn't even six o'clock but we'd somehow missed the dawn. The September morning didn't have the poignancy of autumn; it felt overexposed and hot. I reminded myself that this reality was no more valid than the previous one. Daylight doesn't bring more clarity than night. Sober isn't necessarily the truer perspective.

Twenty years on, I still believe that. But immersion in the mundane can be overpowering. Our Cinderella coach had turned into a pumpkin. Sabine would be ever divine whereas I was just Megan again; I couldn't get beyond the body, the mood, the self. There was a walk, a wait, a train, a bus. As we tenderly parted ways, I tried to think, *This is only the beginning—*

But I knew, even then, it wasn't true.

On shift the following week, things were OK between us but not intimate. It was as if Primrose Hill and all that led up to it hadn't happened. Scanning the papers, I was reminded of what could have gone wrong by the headlines of articles for clients. JOYRIDER KILLS PASSENGERS. FEMALE HITCHHIKER FOUND DEAD. DRUGS DEATH AT PARTY.

In the photocopying room, casting hurt gloom on our night, I showed Sabine.

Her blue-black eyes flashed. "This makes me angry, how they write. A whole person's life is, what d'you call it?"

"Eclipsed?"

"Yes, eclipsed, by how it ends. A tragic death doesn't mean a tragic life. You might have a beautiful life with ten minutes of tragedy in it. But if you die like that, it's a beautiful life forgotten. Everyone thinks only of the end."

She was agitated; her English was halting, her hands trembling as she lit a cigarette. "The ending is not the whole story."

I didn't know what to say.

I imagined she was thinking of her brother, Xavier.

Then she said, "If I die in some horrible way, Meggie, please tell people: it's not the whole story."

PART V

37

Now in middle age, I wonder about the weight of endings. Why should the way a person dies color the memory of their life? Or does the finality of death alone do it? Sometimes to put aside the disquiet of a night's writing, I stroll along the disused railway line near where I live. My thoughts turn to the amputation of dreams, of potential—a life seen minus anything that might have been.

After my mother died a few years ago, peacefully but without resolution between us, the figure in my mind shifted from threatening to intermittently sympathetic. And then when Thandi died of a heart attack three days later, the image I'd had of *her* one day running the flower shop drew to an equally abrupt end. Just as a sentence comes to a close with a full stop, death fulfills the final requirement of a story, completes it. A life looks different when the ending makes it an entire life.

Yet as autumns past and present converge, I am aware of how temporary endings affect perspective too. On my walks, I come across tiny spiders floating midair. Apparently they travel hundreds of miles by ballooning. At a high point, exposing their abdomens, they release a fan of silk strands; their flight is propelled less by wind than by electric fields. And so I imagine an artist's impression of me and Sabine at the highest point in Camden, more intimate than ever, little realizing that gossamer strands were already spooling out, about to whisk us apart . . .

The last time I bumped into Calvin Janssen was at a Halloween barbecue given by a Jo'burg acquaintance. His trendily shaven head revealed a slightly conical skull. Focusing on the fire, we spoke about his latest design project, his involvement with a local school in Kenya, and his plans to cycle around Vietnam.

While we turned the meat, I realized that Sabine's dismissive words made him seem far less desirable. I felt better about the time he'd said, *Not cool, Meggie,* as if her rejection had balanced us karmically.

Given how their night had panned out, I didn't think he'd mention her. But at the first lull in conversation, Cal said, "Your friend's very beautiful."

"She is." I waited for the self-deprecating follow-up line. *I was punching above my weight.* Or, *I guess she doesn't usually go for guys like me.*

"I felt bad about it," he continued. "She kept texting me. *Let's go for a drink. How about lunch.* But there was no point replying."

"Didn't you fancy Sabine?" I asked, hiding my surprise.

"You're *ve*-ry fond of her."

"Of course I am. She's my friend."

"She's really attractive . . ."

"*Ja*. Enough already, Cal."

"But fucked up, hey?" he said.

I took an empty foil platter from the table, then handed one to him. "What d'you mean?"

The meat didn't look done but, platter in hand, he began to load it.

"She's not natural like you, Meggie. She has to play a situation. I'm not saying it's her fault." He rested the tongs a moment on the grill. "Actually, she reminds me of this pretty girl I knew who'd been abused. A person gets screwed up like that, they can't connect properly. Everything's sexual, everything's about attention."

"That's one hell of a conflation—"

"How?"

"Pretty girls, all fucked up?"

"Look, I didn't mean to offend you. Probably I'm making the wrong connections."

He went back to methodically transferring the chops, marking them with soot. Then he said, "This other girl, though, it was sad. She overdosed every few months. I felt sorry for her. But sorrier for the husband. He was always rushing her to the hospital. One day he came home too late."

The meat was all on Cal's platter. Mine was empty; I felt foolish holding it.

"Did she die?"

"*Jys*, it shattered him."

As we walked across the garden to the kitchen, I said, "Sabine doesn't do stuff like that, Cal. Overdosing, or whatever."

He said that wasn't what he'd meant. Then he said the other reason he hadn't replied was that he'd started seeing someone else. Also an architect but from another firm. I wondered if he'd gone out to phone her when we were in the dive bar, if he'd been involved with her already then. The two of them were having people for dinner the following Friday. In the kitchen, he perked up. "Meggie, why don't you come along?"

"I suppose you don't want me to bring my fucked-up friend?" I said.

He looked momentarily taken aback. Then he said, "Sabine monopolized you last time. It'd be nicer to see you without her."

I didn't go to Cal and his new girlfriend's dinner party. Nor did I stay much longer at the barbecue. Without bothering to say goodbye to anyone, Sabine-style I simply left.

Back at Earl's, I ran a bath with lavender salts. That Sabine had lied about Cal didn't bother me. I was flattered at her wanting someone I'd recommended that badly—and that she'd felt the need, afterwards, to save face. I hadn't told her about bumping into Graham; my style wasn't to lie, it was to keep quiet. But that wasn't any better.

Stirring the salts around, I couldn't get them to bubble. I

always wanted them to, though they don't. After I poured in the entire box, they wouldn't even dissolve. As I climbed into the tub, the crystals crunched under my feet.

What *did* bother me was the way Cal had spoken about Sabine. Not just what he'd said but hearing it in his South African accent. I tried to think why.

Relationships between people from different countries involve translation. And this I found liberating. But it could also obscure things. One acquaintance's macho South African ways were given the kind of tolerance his feminist girlfriend would never accord a fellow Brit. Another's impressive small-town nonconformism was lost in Soho's mainstream.

Grinding the salts pointlessly against the enamel of the tub, I wondered: If I were Belgian, how would Sabine feel about me? Would we hang out, or would I not be her type? Would she see me as *natural* like Cal did?

And would Sabine still enchant me if I knew the specifics of her life? Not just the town where she'd grown up or the schools she'd attended—but the way her accent sounded to other Belgians, the clues about herself she gave away subconsciously?

The question that troubled me more, though I struggled to fathom why, was how I'd feel about Sabine if she were South African. When I remembered girls at school with similar personalities, I knew we'd never have been close. But perhaps I needed to look at it from another angle.

Letting some of the oversaturated water out, I added more hot and tried mixing again. The girls who'd fascinated me back then had been beautiful, kind, tough, and restrained. Sabine had all of those qualities.

I lay back and tried to pretend the gritty bathtub was a beach.

It wasn't my problem if Cal couldn't see beyond Sabine being *fucked up*. When I'd been with his brother, Cal had brought home only dark, moody, gothy, fucked-up-seeming girls.

But from the dismissive way he'd said *fucked up* at the barbecue, Cal hadn't seen Sabine in the light he'd seen them. He hadn't found her alluring or captivating; he appeared to feel sorry for her while wary of involvement, mindful of protecting himself. With my toes I pulled out the plug.

So Cal had become old and conservative: stuff him.

38

Yet despite my initial reaction, I added Cal's sense of *fucked up* to my understanding of Sabine. When frustration at being myself became too painful, I'd recall it. When I felt I was acquiescing too far, I'd use it to dilute her effect. The words became my first amulet against her, the first time another person had managed to dull her sheen.

The next amulet didn't come through anyone else's perspective.

We'd been drinking since morning with the rest of our crew. I'd taken things slowly for once whereas Sabine had been at it full tilt. By the time we hit the Black Cap in Camden, she was all over the place: stumbling, slurring, bellowing out wrong answers to a pub quiz we weren't playing. *Disneyland Florida! The Queen of Hearts! Seventeen-fifty-fuckish!*

I'd never seen Sabine drunk other than when I was too, and the distance it created between us hurt. It reminded me of when she was asleep, but whereas asleep she was beautiful, this was different. When the pub quiz teams complained, like a mother embarrassed by her usually impressive kid I said I'd take Sabine out, take her home, put her to bed.

As we went down the stairs, she slammed into a bloke coming up. His pints drenched us. He yelled at her and she yelled back. Then she crashed through the doors onto the street.

She wove ahead of me through the early evening crowd. Catching up with her at the bus stop, I said, "Come, Sabine. We're going home."

"Don' wanna go home."

"Back to my place, then."

"'M huuuungry," she brayed.

"Fine." Gripping her arm, I pulled her into a café.

Under a flickering neon sign that read NO SIGNS ON THIS WALL, I ordered two builder's teas and a large portion of chips. I hoped it would bring her down, help equalize us again. But when the chips arrived, she wasn't interested in eating them. Her eyebrow twitched.

"Let's have liver," she said.

185

"No," I said.

"I like liver in blood."

I felt scared. "Stop being such a fucking pain."

"Whaayouwanmetodo?" That twitching eyebrow.

"Eat what's on your plate, Sabine."

She stuffed her fist with chips and squashed them into her mouth. As she chewed, bits of potato leaked out, dribbling down her chin. Appalled, my eyes filled.

"Don't, Meggie." She pressed a fat red napkin into my face. Prying it from her, I tried to wipe her chin.

She flicked her head away and gazed at her reflection in the window. "You must be careful of Sabine Dubreil," she said in her low voice. "She is a bad influence."

I thought of how her mother could make someone feel so shit they wanted to die, of the scarab pendant, of our time in Eastbourne. I thought of her brother's death. I felt out of my depth. Sabine was in a place I couldn't reach.

The sign flickered; her eyebrow twitched.

"Eat your chips," I said. "*Please.*"

Perhaps the fear in my voice got through where nothing else would. Abruptly, obediently, she gobbled all the chips up.

But then things went beyond her control. On the pavement just outside the door, she puked for Belgium. As the staff began to shout, I dragged her away. Took her hand and ran.

We kept running until the fork to Euston or King's Cross. Then we bent to catch our breath. If the chips didn't do Sabine any good, the puking seemed to. When she stood up, the odd twitching had stopped. She looked exhausted but beautiful again. "I need a shower, Meggie."

"Me too," I said, getting a whiff of puke and beer.

"Let's do it at the station."

"Sabine?" I called wearily as she went ahead of me again. "What are you talking about?"

But at King's Cross she led me down some stairs to a corridor beneath the train platforms. Turned out, you could rent a towel and buy sample-size soap and shampoo. She asked for two sets of toiletries and one cubicle key.

In our rucksacks combined we had all we needed. We washed our hair, brushed our teeth, soaped each other's backs and stood under icy water to finish off. Then we creamed ourselves head to toe with her *fleurs blanches sauvages*.

We surfaced onto the street with damp hair blowing in a late autumn wind that was oddly warm. Sabine seemed normal, back to her usual self. The things that would later concern me—the dramatic talk, the twitching brow, the fear then coldness I'd felt towards her, the mark I'd left on her arm from where I'd gripped her too hard—were momentarily forgotten in the crushed scent of the night. *Wild white flowers.*

We were twenty-four and everything seemed possible.

"Studio X?" she said.

"Great minds," I said.

Then I said, "You were telling the others about it earlier. D'you remember?"

187

She shrugged. "So, ask them along. If that's what you want."

39

"Imagine a harem, imagine cheap drinks. A dark room, a symbolic womb. Drugs from the doorman. Imagine, *dsh-dsh* . . ."

Prawn's improvised rap on the Studio X pitch I'd given several months back was embarrassing. The people queuing under the bridge with us looked more suited to a Kenny G concert than what I'd hyped as the world's edgiest club.

Sabine stood a bit apart. Her mood had changed after I'd called the crew; she'd become subdued, sulky, as if here against her will. Was she getting bored of them? Maybe she was also getting bored of me. I tried not to think, too tired to trust my view on it.

When we reached the front of the line, a man I'd not seen before was on the door. He wore a dirty black T-shirt and low-slung gray tracksuit pants.

Prawn nudged me, mouthing, *Drugs.*

The man glared at Prawn, scratching his eczemaed eyebrows. Then he saw Coño. "No entry with that."

"He's well trained," I said.

"Goes everywhere with us," said Sabine.

"Not here," said the man.

"Could we leave him quietly by the door?" I said.

The man shook his head. "I don't want the dog in sight."

"It's cool," said Earl. "I'll go home."

"You're not going—"

"Next," said the man.

"I need to set off at four for Spain anyway," said Earl.

"If you go, we all go," said Sabine.

"Not me," said Prawn. "I'm going in the symbolic womb!"

I felt myself redden. "Let's just leave this whole thing—"

But Earl had yanked Coño across the road before we could stop him. As they climbed on a number forty-eight bus, he waved the dog's paw from the window. She turned her head to watch us as the bus drove off. Once they were out of sight, the night seemed to drop several degrees.

A cross-dresser in transparent heels came over. "You lot in the queue?"

I glanced at Prawn's eager pink cheeks. "Yes."

"Twenty-five quid," said the doorman, holding out his palm.

"How about a Christmas special?" said Sherry.

"Christmas is a month away," said the doorman.

Lizard said, "How 'bout a hundred for the lot?"

"Hundred and twenty-five for the lot," said the doorman.

"Deal," said Sherry.

"That's twenty-five each, Sherry," groaned Lizard.

Sabine slipped out her silver purse, handed the doorman a fat fold of notes, then strode into the club.

As I reached for my money, the man said, "Your friend paid."

"For me too?" said Prawn.

"Chancer," said Sherry.

"For you all," said the man.

"SJ!" called Sherry, running after her into the club.

"Imagine, *dsh-dsh*, free entry," rapped Prawn, as he followed.

But I hung back. Sabine had sorted this; I'd fix the rest. I spoke to the doorman.

"What d'you want?" he said.

"Charlie," I said.

"Wait here."

I waited. After some time, the owner of the club appeared. He was about seventy, skinny, unshaven, hoary. I'd seen him around before. I repeated what I wanted. He rubbed his bristles. "Might be able to get it for you later."

"OK," I said. "Shall I come find you?"

"I'll let you know," he said.

"So—" But he'd started talking to someone else in the queue.

Our crew was at the bar. Sabine was there too, though with her back to them. She was talking to a girl who looked distinctly out of place. First, because she was clean-cut in blue jeans and a white T-shirt; second, because she was a dead ringer for Kate Moss.

Sherry handed me a large white wine.

I drank half of it, then asked the barman, "Have you got tequila?"

"Nope."

"I can see it." I pointed at a bottle.

"Belongs to someone else." He pointed to the name label on it.

"Relax, Meggie," said Sherry. "Get the next round."

"No," I said. "I want to get something now. How about vodka?"

The barman reached for a bottle under the counter. "Eighty quid."

I handed over the cash. "Five shot glasses too, please."

The club didn't have shot glasses so I distributed heavy-handed pourings into plastic tumblers. Four tumblers, because Sabine was still busy with Kate. I waved in her direction but she didn't see. So I said to the others, "Tour time!"

By the side of the bar was the dance floor. It looked like a wedding disco setup. I gulped my vodka. "Pretty ordinary, huh?"

They nodded.

"But come downstairs."

As soon as we were in the basement I was aware of the rasp of damp. "Normally it smells gorgeous," I said.

"Not tonight," said Prawn.

"They burn this special incense—"

"To hide the toilet smell," said Prawn.

"Oh, stop it, you," said Sherry.

The lighting downstairs was glaring. I recalled candles or at least lamps but there were only bare bulbs. A few of the rooms had double beds with plastic-covered mattresses. One had, in addition to a bed, a jumble of sadomasochistic equipment. It looked like a half-assembled home gym. A metal contraption had a piece of paper with *Broken* scrawled across it. The place was seedy, as I had promised, but not in an interesting way. Rather in a threadbare, depressing way.

"And the dark room?" said Prawn.

"Yes," I said. "I nearly forgot."

I led them to what looked like the door to a broom cupboard. I pushed it open. At least the dark room was dark, but nobody was in it. We hadn't yet seen the club cat, though she attested to her existence with a strong smell of cat piss. "This may seem a bit crap . . ."

"Cat piss, *dsh-dsh*," said Prawn.

"But it's the people who make it," I insisted. "They're not here yet."

"We're here, though," said Sherry.

"You said there were sofas upstairs?" said Lizard.

At the top of the spiral staircase, a ruggedly handsome man with a large nose was kissing a striking brunette. A bald man with bold eyebrows was simultaneously occupied with Handsome's tackle. When the brunette squeezed Lizard's butt, I thought the night was stoking up. But Lizard just said, "Pity Earl's not here."

Studio X had been a mistake. Our crew clearly wasn't into this stuff. You had to be into it to see it as I'd done. Aware of how it appeared to them, I could barely remember its appeal myself.

Afterwards, I'd think this was the point where I should have said, *Guys, let's cut our losses and leave.* Instead, I tried to force the evening to slipstream. I poured more vodka and led the way to the chillout area. The sofas were as wide as I'd promised but also tatty and sunken. Prawn stretched out on the nearest one. As Sherry flopped down beside him, the springs made a loud crack. She put a hand to her back, grimacing dramatically.

"Ooooeee," yelped Prawn, "my back, my back."

But Sherry's face stayed contorted.

"You're not joking?" said Lizard.

"No!" said Sherry. "You bloody noodles."

We helped her up, then laid her flat on the floor. She said she got spasms sometimes, then they passed. "Poor you, huh," said Lizard.

"I get spasms too but in my dick," said Prawn.

"I get hernias," said Lizard. "Got two that need to be removed."

"Hernias play up something awful," said Sherry from where she lay.

What was this conversation we were having? And where was Sabine?

Gathered on the floor around Sherry, we were like mourners at a wake. Clubbers coming upstairs began to make their way over to check out the action. Lizard's duty became to chase them away. Mine was to keep the vodka topped up. Then it struck me: we hadn't slept in almost thirty hours. I handed vodka duty over to Prawn and reassigned mine to finding us some Charlie.

After looking in the basement, I wandered up to the dance area. Sabine wasn't at the bar. But I wouldn't ask after her yet. In clubs, we often separated, then came back together again. Maybe we'd just missed each other and she'd already rejoined the crew. Quite likely, she was by the sofas waiting for me. If I just got something good, the night could still perk up.

Making a pest of myself in the toilets, I was befriended by a woman called Katiana. About my age, height, and build, she had toffee skin and frizzy peroxided hair. She was wearing a bum-skimming pink Lycra dress. Yanking me into a cubicle, she offered a bottle lid of GHB. Touched by a response to my drugs quest, even if not the one I'd sought, I swallowed it. At once I felt weirdly spinny . . .

If I passed out it was only briefly. When I came to I was sitting on the cubicle floor. Through the door, I could hear Katiana talking to someone else. I wished Sabine would appear; she could look after me now. Or not look after exactly; I didn't feel bad—I felt pretty good but ve-ry out of it. It'd be nice to leave the club and go back to Earl's, for us to go back together. I took my phone from my bag to text her—but she'd got there first.

tired sorry gone home

Neither of us had ever left the other in a club. Staring at her message, I tried to put the words in a different order. But the meaning was always the same. Clumsily, I opened the toilet door. I hung on to it.

"More, please," I said to Katiana's pink dress.

"I don't have more."

"Not this," I said. "Charlie."

"Can get but I don't have money."

"Don't worry. I have money."

She pulled me to her and I let her kiss me with a madly probing tongue.

Then, arm in arm, we set off. We joined the growing crowd on the dance floor. They were jigging to some repetitive mechanical beat.

"I love this song!" she shrieked.

She grabbed me by the elbows and we whirled about until we fell down. I looked at the legs dancing around me. Silver, bare, leather, satin. A high chant had been added to the beat. It was cycling up, gathering momentum. I shifted my bum back and leaned against the warmly spinning wall. Closing my eyes, I let the music wash over me in great blossoming waves.

Sabine and I were kissing in a wild field out in the sunshine. I felt our mouths, soft and deep and dark and wet on each other. Our tongues were two snails mating. We were biologists who had been there twenty years. Flowers were growing out of our palms. Except . . . the dance music was so loud. Where were we? I couldn't remember. It didn't matter. I put my arms around her and pulled her close. But she felt odd, different, wrong.

"What's your name again?" I said.

"KATIANA!"

Sabine had left. Flaky Sabine. Fuck Sabine.

"The beautiful Katiana!" I yelled as I stroked her brittle cotton-candy hair.

She pointed towards the corner. "Those guys will get you stuff."

Several groups of men were hanging round in the dark. I couldn't see which of them she meant. "Let's go find my friends," I said. "Tell them the good news."

"Soon we'll be getting stuff," I rehearsed as we climbed the spiral metal stairs. "Soon, yeah, soon."

The chillout area was deserted. Or almost: Lizard and Sherry were the only people left. Sherry wasn't lying flat on the floor anymore. She and Lizard were leaning by the banister, waiting.

"Prawn was looking for you earlier," said Sherry.

"We wanted to go," said Lizard, "but didn't want to leave you."

"Though I see you've found a friend," said Sherry.

Katiana shook her head. "Not friends. We're in love!"

"IN LOVE," I cried at the top of my voice.

Sherry's face pressed into a closed-mouth yawn. Her tired green eyes watered at the corners. *She doesn't believe me,* I thought. So I snogged Katiana fully in front of them.

"You're staying, I guess?" said Sherry.

"Yes," I said. Then I thought maybe they were sad because I had a new lover. I gave them each a snog to make up. "LOVE you guys TOO!"

Afterwards . . . I remember dancing in strobe lights with Katiana. Then going to some guys in the corner. And then being with them in a small room.

The room has a torn orange curtain and a beige filing cabinet. A dirty piece of tape stuck to it is coming off. The guys are saying, We can get what you want. They are laughing. I am saying, I want Charlie. But I think I've said it before. Because they say, We can get you Charlie, Mikey, Ben. They laugh like it's the answer to a joke. They carry on saying things I don't understand but I keep laughing to show I do. Some are smoking, putting ash in beer cans. When I ask for a cigarette, they give me one of theirs half smoked.

They put on a screen with a hospital show. The patient has her hair in bunches and flutter-doe eyes. She is on an operating table but it's all a big gangbang. Do it to me, she says to the doctors. Do it to me hard. She is looking sideways from under the poking-out dicks like she's trying to give me a message. I keep staring at her to see what it is.

A guy with muscles so huge it's like he's a blow-up man says, D'you dig that? I say, Yeah, I dig it. A guy with a thin moustache says, D'you want some? I say to the blow-up man, Do it to me, like in the show. He laughs. Everybody looks impressed. I say, Do it to me, again. Can I join in? says a guy with hairy hands and a gold ring. Yeah, you too, I say. And me? says another one. And me? Only four, I say. God-damn, says an older Rasta guy. I feel sorry for him so I say, Stuff it, everybody can take part. You want K first? says the thin-moustache guy. I mistake K for the blow-up man. Yeah, I say. But they stick a key with white powder up my nose. I taste its bitterness at the back of my throat.

I am lying on my belly on a plastic-covered mattress. A man is inside me. A trouser zip grates: another man. I am lying there not moving. Like a thing, not like a person. Then a man presses at the base of my neck. His hand holds around it. He is rough while he thrusts. I can't move but I can feel him. I can feel my body being pounded like it's something being pounded into something else. I use the pounding feeling. I think, Fuck you to lovely and friendly and natural. To every way I've been misunderstood. To every situation I've hated. To everything I've tried and failed. I am in the dark, I am in a hole. I let go, I give up. I am the dark, I am the hole. I am nothing. I let go, I give up. I lose myself.

Footsteps are coming down the stairs. Stomping along, loud, fast, strong. Voices too: a woman's, a man's, another man's, excited, agitated. I recognize the voice of that girl I kissed. Then of the old man who owns the club. Get out, he is saying low and tight. I know he is disgusted, but I can't make my legs walk. Get the fuck out of my club right now, he says. My heart gets the message. It starts to race. Will he lift me up? Will he dump me in the street? Will he dump me in a tip?

Nobody is inside me anymore. I hear a thud like a body hitting the other side of the room. Feet are stomping again, up the stairs, down the stairs. The noise hurts my head. I cover my ears with my hands. Then I realize I can move again. I lift my head and look around. People are staring at me. I am the center of a big fuss. My jeans are down. The girl I kissed pulls them up. The old man says, What're you all looking at? Get out. Out, out.

When they've left, I say to him, I'm sorry, I'll go. He says,

You're not going on your own. I say, I have a friend. We always stick together, like in the song. Where is she? he says. I don't know, I say. He says, Can you phone her? I get my phone out but the screen reminds me: *tired sorry gone home.* Oh, I say, I forgot, she has gone.

Then I am in an old car with the old man. He is driving and the radio is on. Where are we going? I say. He says, I'm taking you home. He says my address, the flat number and the street. Yes, I say, that's my address. It's the address you gave me, he says. His face looks tired and crumpled and sad. You look like Samuel Beckett, I say. I am seeing you to your door, he says. I tell him, Thank you. Then I tell him, I'm sorry about what happened. I tell him, You have an amazing club. I tell him, Don't worry, nobody will know about this. I try to remember the words I've used to describe his club to others. I tell him, Studio X is a true democracy of race and age and gender.

I don't know if he says anything. I don't remember anything else except the smooth late-night radio voices and the old man's profile in the flickering sulphur of the streetlamps and me trying hard to make up to him. Sorry. Thank you. Don't worry. Please. Yes, sorry. It's here. Thank you. I'll keep schtum.

40

The next morning, I told Earl.

He rang from Calais to remind me to water his orchid. When he asked how the night had been, I heard myself say, "Oh, gangbangish . . ."

"*What?*" I told him more; I said too much. And then he said, "I'm coming back."

"Don't, Earl. Please."

"Where was Sabine?"

I stuck my finger in the orchid's soil. "She left."

"But you two look after each other?"

"We do things alone too."

"I'm turning around *right* now."

"Seriously, Earl, please don't."

The soil was dry but it hadn't affected the plant yet. Nine white flowers went up the stem; I counted.

"Will you go to the police?" he said.

"How can I? I asked for it."

"You didn't ask for rape—"

"It wasn't, exactly."

He gave a long sigh.

"This is between us, Earl."

He was quiet. Then he said, "You need to go to the hospital. Get some antiretrovirals."

I turned on the kitchen tap, cupping water in my hand.

"They might ask questions, Meggie. Do you remember the guys?"

"Only bits and pieces."

"Did you hook up with anyone else? Swap numbers?"

I trickled water around the orchid's stem. "I'll go to the hospital, Earl. I promise."

After we'd finished speaking, I felt ashamed. Earl had never approved of my gung-ho attitude and now this. I shouldn't have told him. Everything seemed worse than before; the words made it seem shocking. Had I used the wrong ones? Had I used the right ones?

I fished about in my sunflower rucksack. As usual, there were scraps of paper with phone numbers from *new friends*, people I'd have chatted to briefly while high. *Call me, definitely, we must go out sometime, there's this other club . . .*

To appease Earl's voice in my head, I began to call around. Every person I spoke to wanted to get off the line as fast as if my words were burning them. I left Katiana until last. Her voice when I got through was disturbingly high-pitched, childish, out of it. "I dunno what the fuck you on about. You expect me to know? Dahling, I don't even know who you are. You the one with the pink hair?"

"I'm the one fucked by a million guys," I said.

"Ooooo," she said. "That one."

"D'you remember anything about them?"

"Two were North African."

"That's a start," I said.

"From Cambodia, dahling."

"Cambodia's not—"

She hung up and wouldn't answer when I called back.

I put my clothes and bedsheets in the wash on a ninety-degree cycle. Then I took a long, scorching-hot shower. Using a worn nailbrush, I scrubbed every part of me.

When I was done, I felt brittle. I needed to be with someone outside the judgment zone. I needed Sabine. Arriving at the Mayfair flat uninvited, I buzzed the intercom. She didn't respond. I waited. Though she dropped round Earl's whenever she felt like it, I'd never done the same.

I looked up at where she'd pointed. Second floor, right corner: a light went off, another went on. For a moment I thought I had the wrong window. But then I saw Sabine's silhouette against a red lampshade. She was in there. I waited longer.

Perhaps the buzzer was broken. I didn't bother with texting; I called. Her mobile rang and rang. I tried a second time, a third. After that it was engaged. When I finally got through, she didn't pick up. I buzzed a *rat-a-tat-tat* on the intercom. Then I pressed my thumb on the button and held.

A concierge in a maroon-and-gold uniform appeared. He asked if he could help. I told him I was trying to get hold of Sabine Dubreil. He buzzed her using his own intercom system with the same result.

"Never mind," I said. "I'll wait."

"Sorry, you can't do that," he said. "You have to leave now. The residents don't like people hanging around."

Although he'd spoken apologetically, as I strode from stupid up-its-own-arse Mayfair, tears squished out of my eyes. Brushing them away with my fists, I spelled everything I saw backwards. I walked quickly but aimlessly until I found myself spelling *latipsoh*. I went in and got a ticket at *noitpecer*.

Being in a place where out-of-the-norm was the norm grounded me. The plastic chairs, the silent subtitled TV, the crisp and soda can machine. When my turn came to see the nurse, I explained the situation. I kept to the facts, then got to the point. "I'd like some antiretrovirals."

"Did they ejaculate inside you?"

"Don't think so."

"Have you showered or washed since?"

"Yes."

"And your clothes?"

"In the machine. Ninety degrees."

She shook her head in disbelief. "You should have gone straight to the police. We can't do anything until you've reported it."

As I stood, my chair fell over.

"You can do it from here," she said.

Pretending I hadn't heard, I strode off along the corridor, then exited through the wrong door. I found myself in a yard filled with hospital bins. The nearest had a label that said FOR INCINERATION. From my rucksack, I took the phone-numbered slips of paper and disposed of them. I looked at what else was in the bag. Keys, purse, and phone fitted in my coat pockets; the Jean Rhys novel too.

"Yo, what're you doing?" a porter hollered.

I dumped the rucksack with the rest of its contents into the bin. I pictured the Marilyn lipstick, the compact mirror, and the cheap skull lighter that I'd bought in imitation of Sabine's, all melting.

The porter started across the yard but I slammed the lid down—and ran.

Parking lot, street, pavement, tar. Fleeing through the city, I dodged people and vehicles as if I were in a computer game. By a designer boutique, I almost collided with a stiletto-heeled woman laden with packages.

"Watch your step," she rasped.

To prevent the leakage of any more tears, I pushed myself to run faster, to go as fast as I could.

I was sprinting, I was numb.

41

When Sabine rang that evening, I let it go to voicemail. She left a message, which, admittedly, was more than I'd done. *Sorry to miss your calls. I'm in Belgium. My mother needed me to go home. Speak soon.*

She'd never spoken of Belgium as home or of her mother other than disparagingly. If Sabine was away now, she hadn't been earlier. But I suspected the reason behind her excuse, and the cause of her anxious tone, was my pursuit of her.

It was understandable that she'd been alarmed by my behavior at the Mayfair flat. How could she guess at what had happened in the club? I'd never gone to her place uninvited before; I didn't phone her, didn't even initiate conversations by text. Had I left a message explaining, we'd have drunk horrible French tea together and she'd have been kind.

But what sort of message should I have left? I replayed hers. *Speak soon* meant, I don't give a fuck why you rang. It meant, I'm not going to risk a conversation with you by asking. It meant, *back off.*

I was upset. Why did I always have to see things from her side? This was the only time I'd ever needed her. Why didn't she trust me enough to know that?

After Studio X, I shut the door to all thoughts of Sabine, self-pity, and dwelling on the past. Though Earl knew what had happened, I didn't tell anyone else. Yet while shame strengthened my inner resolve, my body began its own quiet rebellion. At first it wasn't with any serious illness but a chain of minor physical failures: a couple of colds, then infections that wouldn't heal. Whatever went wrong, I never missed work. When my GP said, *Rest up, slow down, take it easy*, I laughed. What could happen to a twenty-four-year-old with an infection in London? A day later I was hospitalized with cellulitis. It knocked the laughter right out of me.

At the time, I'd just finished three weeks of nights, the

extra one Sabine's idea. After my display of neediness, we were continually on different shifts. Then one night she sent a text: *lets work 3 weeks in a row lets go to brazil.* I replied: *yes lets.* Despite knowing what she was like I persisted in building *castelos* in the air. But halfway through the gruelling stint, she jetted off to Guadeloupe.

When I got ill, I didn't even consider telling Sabine. Earl had made a deal with his opposite to extend his time in Spain by two months, so I didn't tell him. Given that calls to my mother were minimal, I hardly needed to reintroduce drama there. Because I wasn't in touch with the rest of the crew except through Earl, I didn't tell them. Since it was ages to go before my next shift, I didn't need to tell anyone. And I didn't.

Lying in the hospital bed, I couldn't be bothered to read or listen to music or watch TV. Mostly, I stared out of the window at a yellow brick wall. If I died, nobody would notice until January when I was due back at work. Even then, they'd probably assume that I'd found another job. I wouldn't be the first nightshifter to disappear without warning. The shift leader might make a screwed-up newspaper voodoo doll and stick pins in it.

Discharged on the day of the winter solstice, I went home alone. I got in touch with nobody, and nobody got in touch with me. The blackout cloth still covered my bedroom window and I left the curtains in the other rooms drawn. Half the light bulbs in Earl's flat blew but I hadn't the energy or inclination to replace them. I lit candles until my lighter fluid ran out.

Although there was no fresh food, going to the corner shop seemed too much effort. Christmas passed while I huddled under a red blanket on the fake zebra-skin rug in the front room. I boiled rice and ate it with UHT boxed milk. My days went by watching shadows edging each other across the walls.

At midnight on the eve of the new millennium, my phone beeped with texts. Everybody was out having a good time with someone else. Sherry was in Grimsby clubbing with her nieces. Lizard and the shift leader were watching fireworks on Arthur's Seat. Earl and Coño were somewhere on the Costa Brava. Prawn sent a text too incoherent to begin to decipher where he was. And Sabine, typically, sent a text that was blank. I imagined her under a palm tree in Guadeloupe. Or who knows, maybe she was with Lucian at the Ritz.

I ignored all the messages.

Curled up on the rug, I tried to ignore the voices in my head too. I needed to drown them out, to replace them with new ones. Since we didn't have a radio or TV, I fetched my computer to get on the internet. The dial tone sounded and the modem screeched but the server wouldn't connect. Switching it off and on, I unplugged, replugged, and tried again. Rumors were rife about a computer virus triggered by the numerical shift to 2000. But in the early hours of the morning my internet connection came through.

The first radio station I found was in Canada. Listeners were calling in with resolutions for the new year, the new century. I turned the sound down low and opened another tab. Searching for cheap holiday deals, I looked at photos of crowded beaches, built-up resorts, and waterslides. A caller from Winnipeg said she wanted to learn Cantonese. I switched from the Canadian radio station to a Cantonese one. What was the cost of a flight to Hong Kong? Expensive. I looked up learning Cantonese, and browsed other adult education courses. The idea of returning to English literature seemed like a backwards step. Then I came across an introductory writing workshop. But it ran on Thursday afternoons; I couldn't attend day classes while doing nights. Closing all the tabs, I quit the browser.

In my bedroom, I pulled down my blackout curtain. Dawn hadn't yet come but a faint blue light was pressing at the horizon. After putting paper in my printer, I opened a blank document in Word. It seemed like a long time since I'd sat before an empty white screen. I typed my address at the top of the page. Then the press agency's address beneath it.

Then: **Letter of Resignation for Megan Groenewald**

42

I scarcely saw Sabine at work in January. By the start of February, I had a new job in a second-hand bookshop. Since it was in north London, I got lodgings in a retired artist's house nearby. The creative writing workshop I'd found online was full but I joined the local gym. I lifted heavy weights in a series of slow, controlled repetitions. My body didn't change but the workouts helped me feel like I was developing stability and strength.

I didn't hear from Sabine for the whole of February. By the time March slid into April, I assumed the friendship had fallen apart of its own accord. After I left a few texts unanswered, I lost contact with the rest of the crew too. Sometimes I felt a well of sadness that I hid shelving books in the stockroom. More often, I was overcome by a sort of mental exhaustion; Studio X and Sabine and nightshifts were all linked together in my mind.

That spring, I gave my Sabine-style clothes away to charity. I took to wearing cheap combat trousers and tank tops. My sole accessory was the sard ring that I'd bought on Portobello Road. Apparently sard came from volcanic rock and was used to deflect bad spells. As for my more abstract amulets against Sabine, I was almost disconcerted at how little I needed them.

A major contributing factor was the retired artist. She was nonconformist, empathetic, and politicized. I wasn't sexually attracted to her, but I respected her. I didn't want to be her; I wanted to learn from her. Observing how she lived in the day-to-day, I saw, close up, the workings of an intellectual life. In our conversations, I hung on to what she said. I wanted to be someone she'd respect too.

The only regression of those first months was a dream I had in which Sabine was drowning. We were out on open water. I was on a raft but a powerful current was separating us. Though I had an oar, I wasn't using it; I was watching her but somehow not moving. When I awoke, I was overcome by cold waves of sorrow and guilt. But as consciousness returned, I became angry with myself. Why was I feeling bad? In life, *I*'d been the one drowning.

When the artist noticed my blues the next day, I gave her an account of Sabine so reduced as to be barely true—though her response was profoundly useful. She described an experiment where rats were given a pedal to press for a reward. Half were rewarded logically, the other half randomly. Over time, the logical group continued to be logical whereas the random group lost all control; crazed, they pressed the pedal increasingly feverishly in hope of reward.

While the rat aspect was only one part of my relationship with Sabine, it helped with my resolve. I needed a clean break; any leniency would suck me back into our game. Over Christmas I'd sunk as low as I could go. For survival's sake, I couldn't afford to be drawn into Sabine's orbit again.

In mid-April, the magnolia tree outside the second-hand bookshop was coming into bloom. The leaves were light green furls, the yellow flowers startling against the charcoal branches. One afternoon as I arranged a couple of cuttings in a flame-red vase, my phone buzzed with a text. It was written in Sabine's usual style, as if nothing had changed: *want to meet at the pig and hen tomorrow at six.* Compulsively, my fingers itched to type *yes*—but I resisted.

Getting more messages from Sabine over the next few days, I felt bad, as if I'd turned into one of the rat controllers. Then I thought of what Cal Janssen had said about replying when there was no future in it: what's the point? Sabine had so much pride; she was bound to give up sooner or later. But when, instead, she rang and left a voicemail in an urgent tone, I couldn't ignore her anymore. I returned the call. She said she needed to speak to me. She asked if we could meet. I agreed.

Sabine had suggested a loud pub at King's Cross station. My plan was to drink sparkling water, but when I arrived she was in front of two large white wines. Earl's dog, Coño, was at her feet, but that wasn't what caught me off guard. It was her appearance.

She'd never had an ounce of fat to spare but now she was skeletal. Her collarbones protruded from the top of her black shoestring dress. Her chest seemed to cave inwards, her lips were tinged blue, and her skin was chalky. Despite it being late spring, she hugged a thick duffel coat around her.

"Sabine, what's wrong?" I said.

"Nothing."

"You're too thin."

"I lose my appetite," she said irritably. "It happens. Then it comes right again."

"A few months ago, you were fine—"

"That's what you think."

I considered my time in the hospital, then in the flat. "Are you ill?"

She pushed one of the glasses over to me; her nails were bitten to bleeding.

Coño barked.

"Are you looking after her for Earl?" I asked.

She narrowed her eyes. "He said, *Why not take Coño for a bit, now that Meggie's never around?*"

"That's not fair."

"No?" She took out her phone, glancing at the screen. "Can you walk with me to St. Pancras? I need to get the nineteen thirty-nine to Paris."

"Sure," I said.

She downed her wine, then said, "Drink."

I shook my head.

"C'mon, Meggie . . ." She smiled.

After downing my wine too, I followed her across the concourse to a back exit. Behind the building, I felt disoriented. The streets between King's Cross and St. Pancras were deserted. The Channel Tunnel was being extended, both stations refurbished and connected. The blocks around us had become demolition or construction sites. Cranes, gaping holes, rows of metal rods, and scaffolding.

Sabine stopped under the sulphurous light of a streetlamp.

I gave Coño a scratch between the ears and she growled at me. *Yeah, I deserve it*, I thought. I hadn't been in touch with Earl for months either.

When I looked back at Sabine, her eyes were wet. She'd

never cried in front of me before. Reaching out, I touched her sleeve. I felt the coarse material of her coat, her arm buried like a twig inside.

Clumsily, I grabbed the bulky black folds. I pulled her to me and held her. She was so insubstantial that it felt like holding someone else. But when she gave me that look, her dimpled half-smile . . .

Despite my intentions, we started to kiss.

Immediately it felt wrong. Our movements were the same but her breath had the sharpness of fasting. Her saliva was bitter and metallic; her boniness was disturbing. We'd never kissed without an audience, and I wanted to lose myself in it. But I couldn't.

Sabine broke away, tossing her head. Flecks of yellow light reflected in her eyes. Her face became closed, distant. "Goodbye, Meggie."

I stared at her.

Then she said, "That's it. We're done."

Everything was over.

And in that moment, I saw her again as I had in the office when I opened my eyes and she was *there*. Fascinating, free, unreachable . . . and way beyond anything I'd ever be.

I was just somebody who'd followed her for a short while. Somebody whose hand now reached out and slapped her face. Hard.

Her cheeks colored. "What was that for?"

She slapped me back but a play slap, a kitten slap.

My cheek didn't sting but my eyes did.

"Why d'you leave me in the club?" I heard myself say. "These guys—"

"It's always *these guys*—"

I stared at her. "What?"

"You get out of it, and then you're absolutely—"

"And you can talk, Sabine?"

"With you, it's different. Like Earl says, you don't respect yourself."

"Really?" The night slowed down. "What else has Earl said?"

"Nothing, Meggie." She looked confused, then concerned.

"Don't pretend to care, Sabine. Where were you that day?"

"What day?"

"After the club—"

"I told you, I left a message. My mother asked me to go home."

I shook my head. "I saw you in the Mayfair flat."

"So you were spying?"

"I needed you!"

"Why couldn't you just say?"

"Like you *just say* things? *Let's work three weeks in a row, let's go to Brazil?* And then you disappear."

"You didn't want me, Meggie. Already by then you had decided."

I clenched my fists. "For a year and a half, *I* have fitted in with *your* life, Sabine. With how you led it. With what you wanted."

"Is that true?"

"Yes."

"What do you know about me after your *year and a half*?"

My breath was uneven; my head throbbed.

"You used me," she continued. "Used, then dropped. Like you dropped Graham—"

My arm went back intending another slap. But my fist was tight, my body was tight. I swung at her full force.

She turned but into the punch. My ring hit bone. Her head kept moving with the impact but she didn't stumble or fall.

There was a pause. Stillness.

What have I done?

Slowly, she looked back at me.

Blood was coming from her mouth. She swallowed several times. She put her hand to her jaw, stroking it. Then she laughed.

Coño began to bark, straining at her lead. She whined until Sabine gave in to her. Together they headed away, towards a footpath through the construction site.

I watched them go with my heart thrashing.

Then Sabine stopped and turned back.

She threw something, calling, "To remember me by."

After she was gone, I bent down and picked up what had hit me.

It was a tooth.

PART VI

PART IV

43

For two decades I've kept her tooth in the heart-shaped box.

Glancing up at where I've put it, I take a sip of cold coffee and carry on. Typing has become the sound that soothes me most on the nights I can't sleep. It's like I'm trying to crack a code; the light taps are the different combinations. I don't know what I'm doing. But a few moves forward, a few back, I keep on.

King's Cross was the last time Sabine and I were together. Though I was also never again free of her. She became part of the fabric of my mind; a line of the music in my head; a color, the color blue, whenever I saw it. Because of her, I learned French, even lived with a French partner near the border of Belgium in the Ardennes. When the misconceived relationship ended, I stumbled into a job as a freelance translator; over the years, it turned into a career.

Yet Sabine was more than in the language, the subtle tonalities, the pulse of what I was, what I had become. Ideas of her life continued to influence me long after we lost contact. The nature of the influence shifted according to the various endings, like ledges, which I assumed she'd scaled or fallen to.

Once, I thought I saw her at Piccadilly Circus. I was thirty-two, so she would have been the same. Standing by a bin, she was eating a greasy pastry. Her appearance had changed. She was thick-waisted and heavy-limbed, her hair dyed a prematurely middle-aged burgundy; even her elfin features seemed broader, coarsened. She wore a fake fur coat and makeup that looked gaudy in the daylight. Discarding the wrapper, she slurped from a paper cup and belched. When she tried to squash the cup in the bin, it wouldn't fit. She checked to see if a woman a few paces away had noticed.

Her companion had red sneakers, splayed legs, and a sweater with a giant yellow M&M on it. She watched sullenly as Sabine licked the grease from her fingers. Thick flakes of pastry caught in the faux fur of her coat's collar. As she turned her head, slowly, like an injured animal, I withdrew into the doorway of a sports shop. I allowed myself to be pushed past several rails of luminous polyester T-shirts before elbowing my way out.

By then, Sabine had left. Gone.

Just as in nightmares in which I start by whispering "help," then escalate to a shout, I called, quietly at first, "Sabine," then louder, "SABINE, *SABINE*!"

Amid the honking of buses and cars, I ran across the intersection. Shoving through a crowd mesmerized by a beatbusker, I climbed the steps of the Shaftesbury Memorial Fountain. From the top, I scanned the streets for a black coat alongside a giant yellow M&M sweater. Both had disappeared.

Later, I felt guilty about what Sabine appeared to have become. Had my violence towards her been the start of it? Yet along with guilt, I nursed a shameful sense of schadenfreude. I went home grateful, so, so grateful, that my new partner was a neat, normal man rather than a giant yellow M&M sweater person. Though we'd been on the verge of splitting up, I stayed with him for another five years. Or to be more accurate, I stayed until I came across the next temporary ending to Sabine's story.

Although I'd googled her on and off plenty of times and found nothing, one night I located her name in an interview on a personal travel blog. She was a diving instructor in the Cayman Islands. Her girlfriend owned a bar on the beach. In a photograph, the two of them clasped hands. Sabine's eyes were covered by bug-eye dark glasses but she looked no different from when she was twenty-three. Her tooth was fixed and they were grinning into the camera like mischievous kids. The sun was going down behind them over a clear stretch of aquamarine.

My tired eyes hurt; my heart limped with great thuds. So, I'd got it wrong about Piccadilly Circus. So, she hadn't been sexually complex; she'd just not fancied me enough. So, she'd left anything fucked up with men far behind. She'd found herself a fairy-tale ending after all.

I don't believe it was mere coincidence that shortly afterwards my neat, normal partner and I split up. The idea that Sabine had grabbed at something out of the ordinary made me long to have the courage to do the same.

Except, I didn't. We had to sell the flat we'd bought to-gether. Then a significant translation project came through. In a stroke of luck, I managed to rent the newly converted loft above the artist's place where I'd lived before. Now eighty-seven, she was as inspirational as ever. But though for a time my guilt about Sabine subsided, I still somehow couldn't find the energy to truly change my life.

44

Last January, I enrolled in a creative writing course called "Release Your Creativity." Classes were held in a local church crypt and the tutor was enthusiastically dippy. Since I hadn't ever released a sentence that wasn't a modification of some-one else's, I reckoned there was nothing to lose.

At the fourth or fifth class, we were given newspapers to scan. The idea was to tear out anything that snagged us without bothering to question why. We were supposed to do the exercise through the eyes of a character we'd invented. Determined to keep things impersonal, my character was a cyborg sex worker called Capucine's mechanical cat called Tom. But what stopped me halfway through my stack had nothing to do with either of them.

It was a short article about a woman found dead in her home in Peckham. Police estimated that she had been dead for seven months. She was only discovered because new neighbors wanted to ask about an adjoining roof leak. The woman was believed to have been forty-four at the time of her death. Given the body's state of decomposition, it was impossible to determine what had killed her. The condition of the house indicated that she might have been a hoarder. Originally from Belgium, she'd lived in London since the late nineties. The online retailer thought to have been her last employer was unavailable for comment. A colleague from a previous place she'd worked at, Denton Ink Cartridges, said of her, "She was a smashing girl. Pretty, funny, caring, popular. She remembered our birthdays. She made us these great cards. I can't believe this happened to her."

I excused myself to go to the toilet. In the cubicle, I looked up the story on my phone. It had broken a week ago and was repeated in several online sources. One showed a photograph of the staff at Denton Ink with a circle around a pale woman with short black hair. Another had an obituary-type last line: *She is survived by her brother, Xavier Dubreil.*

Sabine was dead. Her brother was not. Never had been.

As I left the church the afternoon turned dark, blustery, and cold. Bare trees lined the pavement like bony hands grasping for the sky. Segueing off into the privacy of an empty common, I listened to the swish of damp grass.

I wondered about Sabine's beach bar girlfriend. What had happened to being a diving instructor in the Caymans? I thought of an idea I'd had more recently, perhaps not an idea so much as a dare, to get in touch with her. Of the wasted hours I'd spent swinging indecisively between whether to or not, thinking about what I'd say to her—when all the while she'd been dead. Lying dead, with nobody even aware of it, in a house in Peckham.

Despite having been teetotal for years, when I got home I cracked open a bottle of whiskey. Then I trawled the internet again. There was no additional news on Sabine's death, nor anything regarding the Cayman Islands. Though I did find a photograph of her in a black swimsuit, hair streaming, bare-faced, pulling herself out of a lido.

She looked like a little girl; I desperately wanted to hug her. Remembering her lie about her brother, I felt stupid for trying to be like her. I thought of her being a hoarder, of her not wanting me to visit her place, of the fear it must have evoked in her. More than ever, I wanted to befriend her again, to do better by her. Of course she'd made birthday cards for people at work. That was what she was like. I missed her in a way I'd never allowed myself to before. She looked so alive.

Folding my arms on the desk, I buried my head in them.

When gray daylight woke me I remembered why I'd stopped overdoing it with the booze. Not the headache or the nausea but the anxiety. Huge, as if I'd accidentally killed someone. I plugged the charger into my phone. A client wanted a video conference at eleven about an art catalogue. There was also a missed call from a number I didn't recognize. The caller had left a voicemail. "Meggie, this is Earl from back in the day. Found you through your translation site. Don't know if you've heard, and sorry to break the news if not, but SJ died. There's a funeral tomorrow. Her bro from Japan asked me to tell those she used to work with. I'll text the address. Hope you can be there."

45

If Sabine had been taller, about forty, and tanned berry-brown, if Sabine had been male with brown-black eyes and no squint—then she might have looked something like the man who stood alone in the front row of the crematorium.

I'd arrived late. Somehow I'd managed to get lost. To think I had the wrong crematorium and cycle to another one, only to have to cycle back. The small hall was overheated and stuffy. None of the people there looked like those I'd have imagined in Sabine's life. Most were middle-aged and older, conventionally dressed. I vaguely recognized a handful from the Energy office, a few more from even further back when we'd worked days.

The speaker at the lectern was scrawny and balding, with a gray beard. He was reading an obscure text that, having missed the first part, I couldn't make sense of. I didn't think it was religious; there was no mention of God, although it addressed the listener as "Brother," and had a religious tone.

I slunk into the back row next to Sherry and Earl. Sherry's hair was still gray at the roots but the rest was ivy-green and shaped in a pompadour style. She didn't look that different in her sixties to how she'd looked twenty years ago: still like an old child, pretty much. Earl's hair was grown out into a statement Afro and he was wearing an olive pin-striped suit that comprised trousers with a sort of straitjacket. It wouldn't have been right for everyone but he pulled it off. He passed me a hip flask. Assuming it contained vodka, I took a hefty gulp. It was so strong that I almost spat it out. He patted my back, more as if to say "well done" than to stop me choking. The afterburn spread through my body; I felt as if I were being illuminated. Sherry smiled while dabbing her puffy eyes with an embroidered hanky.

I stared at the dark wooden casket. Mauve lilies lay on top of it. I could almost hear Sabine say, *The color of the old ladies' hair.* Her soft, low drawl. I thought of the satin inside the casket. Sabine laid out on the satin. Like a jewel. Not like a jewel: she'd been dead seven months. Like something un-bearable to think of, that had nothing to do with her.

When the service was over, a few phrases of piano music tinkled through the air. Then it stopped. I realized it wasn't a recording; there was an upright piano in the crematorium. I shifted to get a better view. The man who had been at the front adjusted the stool and started again. He played with a light, effortless touch.

The red velvet curtains at the foot of the casket parted.

The music was almost sentimental but not quite. Simple, repetitive, sweet, it seemed distantly familiar to me, though I couldn't place it. I was sure I'd never heard it from Sabine. It wasn't her type of music. I thought of my embarrassment when she'd bobbed her head to the start of Prokofiev's *Romeo and Juliet*.

The casket slid towards the curtains. The idea of Sabine being inside it felt forced. The ideas of Sabine being a hoarder, of Sabine having a brother who was alive, those were foreign enough. But Sabine dead? And dead for seven months? The words, the place, the music, the coffin: I struggled to connect them with the person I thought I'd known.

The coffin slowly slid through the curtains.

When the music ended, the crematorium was quiet. I'd asked Sabine once, *What music would you like in the afterlife?* She'd said, *Silence.* I wondered if she'd told the man at the piano something different. He smoothed a piece of navy felt over the piano keys and, gently, put the lid of the piano down. I felt strangely moved by his delicate tribute.

The red velvet curtains closed and the coffin disappeared.

The pub closest to the crematorium had green carpet tiles, a wall-mounted TV, and an imitation antique clock with hands stuck on a quarter past three. Unlike the White Hart, it didn't have a plastic pink stag's head festooned with fairy lights above the bar. Nor did it have a jukebox. But it had a fruit machine: two apples in a row next to a number seven.

"Have a go?"

I turned to see the pianist next to me at the bar. He had something of Sabine's drawl, though his voice was deeper and louder. "I was wondering who'd come here in the mood to play," I said.

He cocked an eyebrow. "Sabine would. She could never resist fruit machines."

"You're her brother?"

"Yes, my name's Xavier. And you are?"

"Meggie."

"Nice to meet you, Meggie." After getting a large red wine, he moved off.

With three of the same, I headed back to Sherry and Earl. We clinked our glasses. "SJ."

There was a silence.

Then Sherry said, "Can you believe nobody missed her in seven months?"

"I hadn't seen her in about twenty years," I said.

"Ditto," said Earl. "Big city. People move on."

"Still," said Sherry. "Nobody."

"It's easy to fall off the grid," said Earl. "She obviously had mental health issues."

"Maybe she got involved with an abusive guy," said Sherry. "He isolated her until he was all she had. Then . . ." She slit her hand across her neck.

"She might have been murdered?" I said.

"Murder, suicide. We'll never know," said Earl.

We were all quiet, chastened.

Eventually, I said to Earl, "It's strange to see you without Coño."

"She died seven years ago in February." Earl rubbed a knuckle in the corner of his eye.

"How?" I said.

"Canine bloat."

"I'm sorry, Earl. She was a great dog."

"Her greatness lives on in her daughter," said Sherry.

"What's the daughter called?"

"Also Coño," said Earl.

"Why d'you call every dog Coño?"

"'S a beautiful name," said Earl. "The best."

I drank some more wine. Then I said, "I thought some of the others might be here. Like Lizard—"

"He's gone Mexican," said Sherry.

"Remember the shift leader? She's with him in Mexico City," said Earl.

"Otherwise they'd have come," said Sherry.

"And Prawn?" I said. "Where's he gone to?"

Sherry and Earl exchanged a look.

I said, "Mexico? Thailand? India?"

"The Scrubs," said Earl. "Got three years for dealing."

"Shit," I said.

"It was fucking unlucky," said Earl. "The pigs were chasing someone else. They broke into his flat by mistake. Then their dogs went mad—"

"It's not all bad, though," said Sherry. "He's made some good friends."

"Yeah, we'll see," said Earl. "Good friends can be a problem."

"That's true," I said.

I wished I hadn't said it. I gulped my wine.

Then Sherry said, "Anyway, he'll be staying with us when he gets out."

I said, "Us?"

Earl looked sheepish.

Sherry planted a purple rose of lipstick on Earl's cheek.

"Guess who got lucky," she said.

After Earl and Sherry had left, I sought out Xavier. He was by the window talking to an elderly man. I got myself another red wine and waited at the bar. There were plenty of people milling around but they seemed to belong to another group; most of those who'd been at Sabine's service had gone.

Xavier wore leather brogue boots, charcoal jeans, and a sandy shirt under a brown plaid blazer. Stylish, as Sabine had been. I couldn't hear what he and the elderly man were saying although it didn't seem particularly intense; they looked like spectators commenting on a distant cricket match. Xavier fiddled from time to time with a leather thong around his wrist. Neither seemed in a hurry to end the conversation.

After I finished the wine, I went to the bathroom. I touched up my makeup, refreshed my perfume, and smoothed my hair.

When I came out, Xavier and the elderly man had gone.

Looking up and down the road in front of the pub, I couldn't see either of them. How could they have disappeared? Perhaps they'd visited the Gents while I was in the Ladies. Returning to the pub, I scanned it methodically. A back exit led out into the car park.

There were plenty of cars but no pedestrians.

"Shit," I said loudly. "Shit, shit."

"Need a lift?" said a man's voice.

Xavier was in an old yellow convertible parked by the fence, smoking a cigarette.

"No," I said. "Though I wouldn't mind one of those."

He waved an empty carton for me to see. "The pub has a vending machine."

"OK, thanks."

I turned, then turned back. "I liked what you played. The tune seemed familiar but I can't place it."

"It's a ballet tune," he said. "Ta ta tada tada, ta ta tada tada . . . Often used for warm-ups at the barre."

"You play for ballet classes?"

"Not anymore. I did when Sabine and I were at school."

"She could've been a brilliant dancer."

"Could've been many brilliant things if she'd stuck at them," he said.

"She was forced to stop dancing, though," I said. "Because of her fucked-up feet."

"Yeah. Her fucked-up feet wanted to take her to—now, where was it that time? Goa, I think."

231

I frowned at him. "Then why the ballet music?"

"To annoy her." He stubbed his cigarette out in the car's ashtray. "She'd have appreciated the irony."

"Could I—ask you some things about Sabine?"

He swung open the passenger door. "Feel free."

I climbed into his car. The interior was beautiful, soft saddle leather. Close up, Xavier appeared to be nearer fifty than forty. There were fine lines on his face, silver at his hairline. I wished I'd caught him in the pub. I felt the distinct absence of props. Wineglass. Cigarette. Loo escape. General buzz.

The silence between us lengthened.

He said, "You're wondering how I didn't notice . . . ?"

"No," I said. "I—"

"Sabine went out of contact intermittently. I used to chase her, harass her, but it never really worked. When she wanted to go AWOL, it was best to let her be. She always rang eventually. Except this time she didn't."

I shifted in my seat. "Actually I wanted to ask something else."

"Go ahead."

"Did she ever mention me to you?"

"Might help if you tell me your name."

"I told you in the pub. It's Meggie."

He shook his head slowly. I looked out through the windshield at the wooden fence. A sign read, CAR PARK. PATRONS ONLY. There was a weeping willow on the other side of the fence. An empty children's playground beyond the willow. I heard myself say, "Sabine mentioned you to me."

"Did she?"

"Yes."

"What did she say?"

"That you were dead."

Xavier burst out laughing. "Typical Sabine! What death did she give me?"

I shook my head.

"You can't back out now, Meggie," he said.

"Sorry. I shouldn't have told you."

"It's OK," he said.

"I'm trying to understand things—"

"Maybe I can help," he said. "But you need to tell me the rest."

In a splurge of words, I told him everything I could remember. About his mother kicking him out, about the BASE jumping, and free-climbing, and finally about him diving to his death off a high rock into a deep pool.

When I finished, he was silent.

Spots of scarlet appeared at his temples.

"I'm sorry." I tried to open the door.

But he grabbed my arm. "Sabine needed attention, Meggie. She didn't care what she did to get it. She had these crazy destructive stunts. Everybody gave up on her. They had to because she screwed them over. One, by one, by one. I was the only person in our family who still spoke to her."

"She was very popular at work," I said, shaking off his grasp. "I did nightshifts with her many years back. But I also read about a guy at Denton Ink—"

"Denton Ink? She didn't need to do these menial jobs."

"Menial?"

"The family has properties in London. She was in one when she died. She had everything going for her. She could do anything she wanted. What did she choose? Cartridges? Cutting up newspapers all night? Gluing them back together again?"

"That was pretty much it."

"You said you worked with her?"

"Yeah, if work's what you'd call it."

He gave a deep laugh, unexpectedly warm.

Suddenly I felt as if I could ask him anything. I thought of the photograph of Sabine as a child. The one I'd swapped with mine on the board when I did days. I said, "What made her like that? What happened to her?"

Xavier sighed. "You want to know?"

"Yes."

"This is the saddest part."

"I want to know."

He kept staring in front of him for so long I thought he'd decided not to tell me. Then he said, "Nothing."

"What do you mean, *nothing*?"

"She had a nice childhood. We had a good, stable home."

"Didn't your father leave?"

"When I was seventeen, so she was twelve, our father died. This was a tragedy, it hit her hard. But Sabine's problems started before then. My mother did everything a parent can do for us. Everything and more. Nothing made Sabine like that. Nothing happened to her. Nothing."

Beyond the willow tree, a scrawny little girl with a nest of fuzzy hair ran across the playground and hid in a green metal barrel. "Arabella?" a woman called after her.

Xavier said, "You know what else?"

"What?"

"I am angry with her. *But*—whatever trouble she caused, and Sabine caused massive trouble—I've never had more fun with anybody."

"Me too," I said.

He turned to me as if a thought had occurred. "Were you her girlfriend?"

"No."

He smiled as if he didn't quite believe me. I was glad he didn't.

"Arabella!" called the woman. "Where are you? Answer me immediately!"

"I need to get to a class," I said.

"I'll give you a lift."

"It's fine, I've got my bike." I opened the door.

He took a business card from his glove compartment. "Meggie, many people were taken in by Sabine. I'm in town for another week. If it helps, I can answer your questions. I can tell you everything you want to know. I can even show you some photographs."

"Thanks," I said. "I appreciate it."

He scribbled a number on the back of the card and handed it to me. "Give me a call."

46

We met up the day after the funeral in a large department store coffee shop. Xavier seemed reserved. Then we got lost in the kitchen section coming out, and the mood between us changed. He bought a red-and-white picnic basket on the spur of the moment. Leaving the till, he stared at the purchase as if it had magically appeared in his hand. "Your fault, this," he said.

"My fault?" I said.

"So now, tomorrow, we have a picnic," he said.

It was still very much winter, but the next day I sat on a tartan blanket in the middle of Hyde Park and listened to him until an icy cloudburst soaked us. To make up, the date after that, only four hours later, was in a swanky Knightsbridge restaurant. He talked and talked and wanted to talk more. Despite my ability to speak his language, English suited us both, played to our fantasies perhaps. After the meal, we went to a hotel bar. Then we went to his hotel bar. When it closed, we went up to his suite. And so our affair began.

From the start, all the time that we spent together was punctuated by conversations about Sabine. He needed to talk about her, and I allowed him to think I did too. In truth, his accounts of her bore almost no relation to the person I had known. His stories meandered contradictorily; some recollections seemed fantastical, others surprisingly dour. Once, he put me on the phone to the elderly Irish au pair who had looked after them as children; her descriptions of Sabine as "timid, sensitive, softhearted, and prone to fits of crying" were no more illuminating.

Everybody had their own version of Sabine. With this in mind, I let Xavier's stories wash over me. They were compensated for by the instances when glimpses of Sabine slipped through. His presence could be almost as visceral as hers, as compelling. His gestures had her unpredictable quickness. When he was tired, his brown-black eyes developed a slight squint. I kept him up late deliberately; I plied him with espresso martinis strong on caffeine. And then there was his voice; from the beginning I thought I recognized beneath the boyish boldness something of her timbre. Soon I discovered that if I spoke softly to him, he spoke softly back. Her low, soft tones emerged behind his; soft, low words pulsed back and forth between us.

At night in bed his skin was hot, just as hers had been. Like her, he tossed around and threw the duvet off. Like her, when he slept he seemed sufficient unto himself: solemn, untouchable. Unlike her, when he awoke he drew me to him. He held me so tightly I could scarcely breathe, though I stayed in his embrace for as long as he would allow.

Everything during those weeks we spent together seemed poignantly heightened. I turned down translation jobs. He postponed his flight back to Japan. We often stayed up until the dawn chorus sang us to sleep. We ate dark chocolate for breakfast. We watched films in empty cinemas at midday. We fed the ducks and geese in St. James's Park. We did all the things that lovers do when the city is their playground. Though I knew that it couldn't last, when he asked if I'd move to Kyoto, I said yes.

Only hours later, as I returned to my flat, I got a call from a woman with a Japanese accent. Could I please stop chasing her husband? Could I please leave her Xavier alone? He had promised to be at Akihiko's birthday. Who's Akihiko? I asked. She said, Our eldest son. If Xavi didn't leave soon, he would miss the occasion. Could I please just let him come home?

I rang Xavier the moment I got off the phone but he didn't pick up. When I hadn't heard from him by evening, I blocked his number. Then I blocked his address from my emails and activated a vacation auto-response on my account:

Away for some time. Will reply to messages only intermittently.

I couldn't block my postal address, and it was through the post that Xavier sent his single addendum to our affair. A rectangular package covered in postmarks from Japan. It contained the scarab pendant with *My Sabine* engraved on the back. His note provided no apology, no explanation—just, *I gave this to Sabine. She'd want you to have it. X*

*

After the affair ended, I began battling with insomnia. I started out doing everything you're supposed to do. The things I'd done when I worked nights, updated with contemporary extras. A strict sleep schedule with minimal time in bed. Rigorous daily exercise with no naps. No tea or coffee after midday. Plus sleep stories, hygiene checklists, and soothing meditations on smartphone apps.

None of it helped. The moment I lay down in the dark, I saw Sabine as painfully thin as she had been at the station. The way she had turned her face into my punch. At Piccadilly Circus licking her fingers by the bin. I heard myself ask if a lover had given her the pendant, and her say that was one way to put it. I remembered her face underwater in the Hampstead Pond. I got stuck on morbid last scenes in a way that would have made her angry. But when they weren't at the forefront of my mind, it was worse.

Eventually, I consulted my doctor. She spoke about counseling or antidepressants, or sleeping pills as a last resort. Given my lack of enthusiasm for these options, she suggested focusing on something pragmatic. Insomnia could be your body's way of rousing you to get on with a task. An activity you had previously been blind to, or neglectful of, in your waking hours.

I cleared my desk of French–English dictionaries, soup bowls, and coffee mugs. What I had to do, the shadow thing that had been waiting its turn, was write. I thought of returning to the course in the crypt but sleep deprivation made me a snail needful of my shell; the idea of heading into the city's bustle was about as appealing as a sprinkling of salt.

Instead, when the night withdrew into its quietest hours, I put on my lamp. I sat down in front of my computer. I didn't feel drawn to exploring the cyborg sex worker with her mechanical cat. I needed to write about something that burns in me like phosphorus. Someone I can't extinguish from my mind.

Who else could I ever write about?

I have almost made a story of what happened. Most of what I remember is here, though the memories are continuously shifting. I have my theories about Sabine but that's all they are; she's no longer my Sabine any more than she is yours. As I gaze at a streak of crimson in the slate sky, for a moment I don't know whether it is dawn or dusk. But no matter.

When the thickest part of the night comes around again, I'll sit on the blue silk throw that covers the sofa. After lighting five white tealight candles, I'll smoke a cigarette. Playing some of our favorite tracks, I'll drink tequila toasts. To what can never be resolved: to endings, to Sabine. I will open the heart-shaped box.

And then, when I am ready, I will write the final sentence.

ACKNOWLEDGMENTS

Thanks to:

Matthew Francis for sage advice throughout.

Evan James for open generosity and valued judgment.

Howard Lester and Melanie Newman for insightful feedback; Rachel Mendel who got it from the start; and Heather Dyer and Suzanne Ushie, whom I'm lucky to have in my corner.

Greg Keen for trenchant critique, time and again.

And to my father, Glen Ladner, the storyteller I was so lucky to have as a child.

Also, thanks to Cathryn Summerhayes, my extra-mile agent at Curtis Brown. Ravi Mirchandani for his intuition and vision. Charlotte Greig for her all-round editorial wisdom. Emma Bravo, Grace Harrison, Chloë May, and Roshani Moorjani at Picador for their generous enthusiasm for the book.

In the U.S., special thanks to Molly Gendell, my talented editor at Mariner Books. And to the great team who worked on the book, especially Maureen Cole, Ryan Shepherd, Dale Rohrbaugh, Mumtaz Mustafa, Yeon Kim, Angela Boutin, and Lucy Albanese.

Finally, I am grateful to Aberystwyth University for the Ph.D. funding that gave me the time to write *Nightshift*.

ABOUT THE AUTHOR

As a child, Kiare Ladner wanted to live on a farm, run an orphanage, and be onstage. As an adult, she found herself working for academics, with prisoners, and on nightshifts. Her short stories have been published in anthologies and broadcast on BBC Radio 4. *Nightshift* is her first novel, written while studying for a Ph.D. She grew up in South Africa and lives in London.